Agent Svetlana Simonov of the government's top-secret Omega Force is sent from Washington D.C. to Mexico City to get inside the organization of two of the country's deadliest and most well-protected underworld kingpins—the brothers Rico and Tomas Santiago. They have created a fortress for themselves that is impenetrable by military force. But maybe, if Svetlana uses her all her sensual charms, she can get past their defenses. This is critically necessary because the king-pins have hired three of the finest scientists specializing in infectious diseases in the world. The scientists are working around the clock, and their goal is to unleash this deadly new pandemic virus into the major cities of the United States and Europe.

Working with Svetlana to take down an army of enemies are three highly trained mercenaries, who provide the muscle that backs up Svetlana's charm. Can Svetlana work with three cold-blooded killers she knows nothing about? Can she trust them? Will they trust her? Can she lure the Santiago brothers to let her inside their impregnable fortress?

Svetlana embarks on her most deadly and critical mission with only her stunning looks and cunning mind to defeat a heartless enemy.

A Virus to Die For
Copyright © 2020 Robin Gideon
ISBN: 978-1-4874-3035-1
Cover art by Martine Jardin

Published by eXtasy Books Inc or
Devine Destinies, an imprint of eXtasy Books Inc

Look for us online at:
www.eXtasybooks.com or www.devinedestinies.com

A Virus to Die For
Agent (Rom)antics Book 5

By

Robin Gideon

DEDICATION

This one's for me and Cat and Nicki and Jay and for Martine. Because, damn it, we worked like rented mules to get it out, and had a hell of a lot of fun doing it (okay, regarding that last part, I'm speaking only for myself). Never worked with a better team. Ever. Smooches, girlfriends. (But I hate that I'm not supposed to use exclamation marks in my writing. Just sayin'.) And as a warning to the ladies listed above, be assured that Svetlana is a long way from retirement. (Now you're supposed to hear a diabolical laugh.)

CHAPTER ONE

It was a lovely afternoon, but Svetlana Simonov could not see the beauty surrounding her because of the latest assignment that had been given to her by her commanding officer and lover at Omega Force, Jefferson Burke.

For this assignment she was supposed to work with three mercenaries, hired ex-soldiers from a private security outfit called Security Solutions. All Svetlana was supposed to do was find the scientist working to create a new, even more deadly version of the Coronavirus, and let them know where he was. They'd take care of the rest of the assignment — namely, killing the scientist. How they neutralized the threat was up to them.

It wasn't surprising that Omega Force was outsourcing the dirty work of doing the actual killing. Svetlana knew that she was a honey trap. Eye candy had destroyed so many powerful men over the years. Beautiful women could be more deadly to men than a switchblade knife.

Svetlana knew that one of her main defenses was the fact that almost nobody knew who she was, and she didn't know anyone who worked at Omega Force, with the exception of her controller, Burke, and a young field agent named Tatiana. Her work for Omega Force was entirely off the record, as far as the government was concerned.

She took a sip of her coffee, then picked up the electronic tablet once again. She did an optical scan to get past security, first of her thumb, and then of her entire hand. When the electronic keyboard showed on the glass screen, she tapped in the proper code, and once again the image of three men came up. Svetlana decided the three were good-looking, though they all had that cold-eyed, hollow-cheeked look to them, as did so many men of action, men who knew what it was like to have been shot at and missed, and sometimes shot at and hit.

These were men who wouldn't buckle under the strain, no matter what the situation was like. These were men who had killed before, and would do so again.

The leader of the trio was an American. His dossier said that he was thirty-eight, and had been with Security Solutions for eight years. He had been recruited by Security Solutions upon his retirement from the American special forces. He had served in Somalia, Afghanistan, and Iraq while in the service of his country. While working for the firm, he had done assignments in all three of those countries, as well as Germany, Turkey, Kazakhstan, and Ireland.

Ireland? What the hell would he be doing in Ireland?

She looked at the face on her electronic tablet, and decided that although he was certainly a handsome man—he was tall, blond, and broad-shouldered—he was probably a cold-hearted bastard who cared only about the assignment, himself, and his men. Svetlana suspected that most mercenaries were that way.

Thirty-eight. That's the same age as Burke. I wonder if he has Burke's sexual stamina.

Svetlana immediately dismissed this line of thinking for several good reasons. The first was that she had no intention of ever finding out what the American's sexual stamina was, so it made no difference. Whether formidable or pathetic, Svetlana didn't know and didn't care. The second was that she had been given this assignment immediately upon finishing her previous assignment, without being debriefed by Burke afterward. Part of a mission debriefing by Burke meant a rollicking good roll in the hay that inevitably caused Svetlana to have at least three climaxes, and quite often, many more than that. Once, when he'd debriefed her in Munich over a three-day period, Svetlana had so many orgasms that she had lost count.

She could hardly walk, and she couldn't stop smiling.

It was a fond memory.

Working with Jack was Nigel Harris. He was British, and his military background was with the vaunted SAS. He, too, had been deployed in the finest vacation hotspots on the globe. He was thirty-two. He had no post-high school education, other than what he received from the SAS and Security Solutions.

Svetlana suspected that the kinds of things Nigel knew how to do probably didn't look real good on most resumes — unless you were looking for someone highly skilled at killing people.

The third of the trio was Brad Hays, an Australian. His background was similar to the others, with the exception that he could speak several of the languages from East Asia.

That's unusual. I wonder how he learned those.

Guys like him didn't learn anything just for the hell of it.

Svetlana looked up from the tablet. There were hundreds of people walking, some hurrying, others taking a more leisurely, distinctly Mexican attitude toward the day. They walked at a slow, casual pace.

I'd go crazy if I took a siesta every afternoon.

Svetlana was far too much an American — meaning she was far too ambitious — to ever think that taking a nap in the afternoon was productive behavior.

Looking around at the majestic building of the Hotel Mexico International, Svetlana found it hard to reconcile the stately beauty of her surroundings with the rampant corruption of the government. She hadn't spent much time in Mexico, but when she was there, she was always somewhat surprised at how there seemed to be two countries pretending to be one, all while living in the same house. There were plywood shacks and crushing poverty five hundred yards from villas that even the Beverly Hills elite could not afford. There were stately government buildings, and within those walls, every politician was for sale to the highest bidder. There were vows made to put an end to the corruption and the drug dealing, made by politicians who were owned body and soul by multi-national corporations which had no body or soul, and drug kingpins who treated their children like they were gods, yet had no trouble feeding drugs to children less fortunate than their own.

Svetlana was sitting in the hotel's outdoor café. The people who could afford to spend a night or two at the hotel could afford a night or two anywhere in the world, and most likely, they traveled there via private jet they owned, or borrowed from their best friend, who said he didn't need it for the next few days because he was staying with his mistress.

She saw the mercenaries approaching, recognizing them instantly. All three were wearing department-store off-the-rack suits, government regulation haircuts, and that straight-shoulders way of walking that the military drilled into its young recruits, who never forgot what they'd learned.

They're bigger than the locals. At least three or four inches taller than most of the men around them.

She wondered if that would be a liability for the mission. If Security Solutions had chosen men to fit in with the local indigenous population, they had done a dreadful job of it.

She made direct eye contact with Jack as he walked toward her, and she gave him a smile. He returned the smile, and she was a little surprised to discover that he had a deep and very attractive dimple in his left cheek. It gave him a boyish quality, but he was all man.

"Miss Simonov, I presume," he said. Brad and Nigel moved to flank him like bookends.

Svetlana rose to her feet. She was glad she was wearing five-inch stilettoes. They brought her height to six-foot-two, so she looked the mercenaries directly in the eyes. That was so much better than having to look sharply upward to see into a man's eyes. The only time Svetlana really liked doing that was when she was on her knees with Burke standing in front of her. She always liked it when the Dom in Burke came out and he commandingly put her on her knees.

"You presume correctly," Svetlana replied, shaking his hand. She knew her English had a significant Russian accent.

She shook hands with the other two, who introduced themselves, though Svetlana already knew their names. Since she'd known they'd be coming, she had selected a table with four chairs. When the men sat, the waitress hurried forward. The men ordered a pot of coffee and said they wouldn't be ordering any food.

After coffee came and the waitress had left, Svetlana decided to dispense with any further pleasantries.

"Tell me how long you've been here, and what you've learned." Her voice was clipped. She looked directly at Jack and didn't so much as glance at the other two, making it clear to everyone involved that she knew very well what the power structure was for Security Solutions operatives.

"One week," Jack said. "Mostly what we've learned is that Rico and Tomas Santiago never seem to do anything the same way twice in a row. They have a walled estate about fifty miles from here. They commute to Mexico City every day. They are never without heavily arms guards."

Svetlana sensed that Jack and his men were solid, top-notch professionals, men who knew what their jobs were, and knew how to fulfill their obligations without a lot of help from the corporation's top executives.

"Every day they've got an armada of four armored SUV limousines with blacked-out windows that go from their compound to the city. Sometimes the limousines drive in formation, and other times they split up. With the tinted windows it's impossible to tell which of the brothers has gone where. And with traffic here being what it is, it would take at least thirty cars to try to follow them. That would take way too many men and cars for our operation to remain a secret. Not in Mexico City. In this city, the spies have spies who have spies, and informants inform on informants who inform on their own parents."

"Just the kind of place I make a point of avoiding," Svetlana said, telling the truth, though she suspected she probably shouldn't have let these men know what she was thinking.

"This is the kind of place my boys and I usually find ourselves working in," Jack replied, smiling.

He surprised Svetlana then by picking up the coffee pot and refilling all their cups. It was the kind of domestic courtesy that she hadn't expected from a man of his profession. She wondered what else about him would surprise her.

"I've read your dossiers, and I suspect you've read mine," Svetlana said, adding just a hint more distinction to her Russian-accented English. "What do you know about me?"

"Dual citizenship with Russia and the United States. You speak Russian and English, and have a passing knowledge of Spanish, French, Italian and German. You travel all over the world, and you must have the world's best luck, because wherever you go, people start dying and somehow you're never in the morgue. Other than that, not much . . . other than you're supposed to get inside the compound and figure out where the laboratory is so that we can blow it sky high and kill the scientist who is trying to create the next version of the Coronavirus."

"Very good," Svetlana said. She suspected he really didn't know much more than what he had just told her. Svetlana knew in her heart that Burke would keep the vast majority of her true background a secret.

"How much do you know about Rico and Tomas

Santiago?" Jack asked.

"Their home is like a fortress, and nobody gets in or out, except occasionally women. It used to be a golf course. That's where I come in." Svetlana smiled at them. "Muscle solves many problems, but not ones like this one. To get inside the compound is going to require a lady's charm . . . provided she's not *too* much of a lady."

Svetlana looked away. She had no illusions as to why she had been sought out by Omega Force, and the mercenaries she was with understood exactly what the score was.

"Before you get any deeper involved in this operation, I want to make sure you know *exactly* what you're getting yourself into," Jack said.

Despite the Mexican heat, Svetlana felt a chill go through her. "I'm listening . . . more carefully than you can imagine."

"Rico and Tomas Santiago aren't your garden variety rich men who like the ladies. They're something much more than that."

Svetlana leaned toward Jack. He had started speaking much more softly. Then, just as he was about to resume, four women — all middle-aged and obviously wealthy — took the table beside Svetlana's.

"Maybe we should continue this conversation elsewhere?" she said.

"Suggestions?" Jack asked.

"I have a suite on the penthouse level. We can go there. There's plenty of room, and if we get hungry we can always call down for room service."

"Excellent," Jack replied. "Lead the way."

Jack had seen video images of Svetlana, but as he walked through the lobby toward the elevator, he decided that the images just didn't do her beauty true justice. Today she was wearing a miniskirt and strappy pair of high-heels that put her legs on display. They seemed to go on forever. Startlingly vivid mental images of what pleasures he would experience should she ever wrap those long legs around his hips while they had sex snaked through his mind, and the mental image was so jolting to the senses that he faltered a step.

No wonder she's used as bait. What man in his right mind could resist her?

When the four of them got in the elevator, an elderly couple from some European country did as well, and Jack was glad they did. He didn't want to be alone with Svetlana until he could tamp down stray unwanted emotions, anyway.

She could tempt a monk to sin. She could make any man break his most solemn vows.

"It's this way," Svetlana said once the elevator doors opened when they reached the penthouse floor.

"I've got to tell you, guys like us don't often get up to these floors in hotels as upscale as this one," Jack said.

She used her key card to open the door, then walked in, pushing the door wide. The suite was just a single room, but it was enormous. Jack had never seen such a hotel room. On one side was a six- or eight-person jacuzzi. Not far from it was a mahogany wet bar with countless bottles of liquor behind it, neatly set on theater seating shelves so all could be seen. To the right was a king-size bed, with bedside tables on each side with green shaded reading lamps. There was a dining room table with seating for six. Jack suspected that the closed door led to the bathroom. He wondered how opulent that would be.

"Holy shit," Brad said, "this is incredible."

"It's bloody beautiful, that's what it is," Nigel added.

"Watch your language," Jack said sharply.

"If there's anything you need, anything you want, you just have to ask and it's yours," Svetlana said. "For myself, I'm going to have a cola. They're in the refrigerator, if you're interested. If you're looking for something stronger, there's beer in the refrigerator, and every kind of liquor you can think of is behind the bar."

"Thanks. How about we all sit at the table?"

"Perfect," Svetlana said.

No, you're what's perfect.

The next thing he did was try to forget his previous thought.

He watched as she went to the long table and sat in one of the chairs. When she sat, her miniskirt raised slightly, showing a little more of the backs of her thighs. Jack wondered if she always dressed in such a sexy manner in hopes of bolstering the case for her being on the mission.

He had precisely no doubts whatsoever that she was exactly the right person to lure Rico and Tomas into letting their defenses down so that they would be vulnerable to attack.

When everyone was seated—Svetlana on one side of the table, and the men on the opposite side facing her—Svetlana folded her hands on the table, looked Jack directly in the eyes, and said, "Now let's have all the dirty details of the sex life that Rico and Tomas are inflicting on others. I want to know everything. I want all the nasty details."

"They're not sadists, but they do play a pretty rough game," Jack said, carefully monitoring Svetlana's expression, and any other physical reaction she might have to the information he was presenting. "They like to share one girl. At Security Solutions, our psychological analyst has suggested that there's probably a strong, subliminal taboo-slash-homosexual element involved with what they're doing. They aren't even aware of it, in all likelihood. Since they can't have sex with each other, they share a single girl, and because they're not happy unconsciously with their desires, they make it rough on her."

"Rough?" Svetlana asked after taking a sip of iced cola. There was an edge in her tone. "How rough are we talking here?"

"It's psychological as well as physical. They're heavily into ordering people around, as well as bondage. But as near as we can tell from the interviews we've had with women who have been there, they're not into blood, pain, or any real sadism."

"So they dance on the fringes of the BDSM life, but they haven't jumped in with both feet. That's what you're saying?"

"As near as we can tell," Jack said, measuring his words carefully, "but there is no guessing when they'll decide to take that next step." He cleared his throat. He felt obligated to give Svetlana a full account of the brothers, but this was a dicey subject to talk about with a beautiful woman he'd only met earlier in the afternoon. "If you get involved with them, you'll have to be on guard every second you're with them."

"Don't worry. I've played this game before."

"These men have ordered the assassinations of literally scores of people. Both men and women. They've bought politicians from one end of Mexico to the other. And remember, when I say they like to share their girls, that means they have them at the same time."

He half-expected Svetlana to at least blush at his implications that they enjoyed double-penetration, but all she did was lower her gaze to the table for several seconds, then sip her cola before once again giving him her full attention.

"They like handcuffs, I've been told. And two of the girls they brought to the compound said they're really into pulling hair. Think you can handle that?"

"How long do the girls stay?"

"Usually a week," Jack said, pleased with how this part of the pre-mission briefing was going so far. Svetlana was impressing him, though he still had his misgivings. "Sometimes two weeks. I've never heard of them keeping anyone more than two weeks. The girls just can't take it physically or psychologically. They do, however, get paid very well."

"Two weeks . . . that's a long time to go through something like that, no matter how much money you're making." Svetlana shivered, then pretended she didn't—and that's when Jack knew that he was getting through to her.

"They pay the girls handsomely, but while they're with Rico and Tomas, they're treated almost like slaves—to be bossed in every way you can imagine, and probably in some ways you can't imagine."

Jack watched another shudder go through Svetlana, and he knew at that moment that he had to test her personally before he would feel comfortable sending her out on the assignment.

"Do you know what kind of a role you'll have to play?" he asked. Svetlana nodded. It was a direct response, but not much of one. "Have you ever *been* a slave?"

Jack watched as a blush started in Svetlana's cheeks, and made its way to her ears. For a moment he wondered whether he was testing Svetlana for the mission, or if he was just indulging his own fantasies. One, the other, or both could be true.

Jack rose to his feet. An instant after he did, so did Nigel and Brad. With the briefest of glances at them, he knew that they were all on the same page mission-wise. They had been in too many firefights together to not read each other's mind.

Jack walked slowly around the table, looking at Svetlana as he took each step. He could tell that she was nervous. Very nervous.

CHAPTER TWO

*F*uck. *Now what's he up to?*
Svetlana could feel her heartrate accelerate as Jack walked slowly around the oblong table in her luxury suite. His expression had all the softness of granite. In his blue eyes there was all the movement, warmth, and forgiveness of a glacier.

He didn't stop walking until he was standing directly behind her. Svetlana fought against the urge to look over her shoulder at him. She wanted to ask him just what the hell he was doing, but she strongly suspected that to put voice to such concerns would be *exactly* the wrong thing to do.

Jack's voice was soft but commanding when he said, "Stand up." When Svetlana did as he ordered, he pulled her chair away from her, then stepped behind her once again.

"You've got to learn how to follow orders," he said.

When Svetlana looked at Nigel and Brad watching from the opposite side of the table, she saw the all-consuming fire of lust in their eyes. Even if *she* didn't know, they knew exactly what was going on. She sensed this wasn't the first time the three of them had played this game with a woman.

"When I give you orders, you must follow them instantly. Is that clear?"

"Yes," Svetlana replied. And then, after several seconds, she said, "Yes, sir."

"Good. Now my men and I are going to brainstorm how we're going to get you introduced to the Santiagos. If you simply approach them and introduce yourself, they'll smell a trap and you'll never get close to them again, and you

certainly won't get inside the compound. So we've got to figure out how to get them to approach you. And while we're
figuring that out, you'll pour me a whiskey on the rocks, and
get beers for Brad and Nigel."

Svetlana, in a soft voice, said, "Yes, sir."

As she started to walk toward the well-stocked wet bar,
Jack said, "And while you're at it, get rid of the bra and
jacket."

Svetlana felt the breath catch in her throat at Jack's last
command. She hadn't foreseen something like that happening, but now she suspected that she should have, and for several logical reasons. The first was that if ever there was a man
with a take-charge personality, it was Jack. The second was
that she should have anticipated being tested by battle-hard-
ened men she had never worked with. And the third was that
she was attractive, and the three men had testosterone counts
high enough to get a woman pregnant if she did nothing more
than inhale the air around them.

She walked to the wet bar, stopped, then with her back to
them, she dropped her jacket to the floor, then made quick
work of unbuttoning her blouse. Once she had, rather than
taking her blouse off, she loosened the bra shoulder straps
completely until they were free from the cups, then reached
behind her back under the blouse and freed the hook-and-eye
closure between her shoulder blades. She pulled the bra off
completely, then quickly rebuttoned her blouse and tucked
the tails into the waistband of her miniskirt.

*I've outsmarted him with that one. He'll get his revenge, though.
Men like Jack always do. They always come out on top – and they're
often on top of a woman when they do.*

She made the drink, opened the cans of beer, then carried
the cans in one hand, and the drink and her bra in the other.

"I thought you might want these," she said, handing Jack
both his cocktail and her bra at the same time. She wondered
whether her cheekiness might draw a punishment, and if it

did, what *suffering* she would go through because of it.

As she walked around the table to give Nigel and Brad their beers, Svetlana could feel her breasts moving, wobbling tautly with her steps. She was far too buxom a woman to un-obtrusively go without a bra. To do it now, when she was be-ing watched with unblinking eyes by strong, handsome men who were used to giving commands, was exciting. To be able to feel the smoothness of the silk against her hyper-sensitive nipples was causing the lips of her sex to moisten. There was now a distinct throbbing sensation in her clitoris.

Brad and Nigel made little effort to hide the fact that they were staring at her swaying breasts as she walked. Svetlana stepped between them, slowly and deliberately setting a beer down in front of each man. She knew she was near enough to them for them to smell her Chanel No. 5. She was close enough to their powerful bodies to feel their heat, and her nip-ples and vagina reacted accordingly.

"Now men," Jack said, pushing a laptop computer away slightly so that all three of them could see it, "we know they leave the compound every day at nine or ten, and don't return until five or six, or sometimes even later."

"We assume that's true, but with those tinted windows, we don't really know if Rico and his kid brother are actually in the limos," Nigel said. "They could still be back at the com-pound, for all we know. And when they go to the city, they often go into a garage, so we don't know if either man gets out."

"So how the hell do we get them to approach Svetlana if we don't know where they're going to be?" Brad asked.

"That's the bitch of it, now isn't it?" Jack said, disgust and frustration in his tone.

Svetlana walked until she was standing behind Jack, and slightly to his left. She said nothing, but she listened very care-fully to everything that the men said.

For thirty minutes the men talked, and Svetlana could tell that they had brainstormed like this on missions many times before. On several occasions she wanted desperately to give a suggestion, to let the men know her opinion on something, but she kept her tongue silent. She was being given a test by them, and it was one she intended to pass.

"Svetlana, I'd like another whiskey, and Nigel and Brad need beers," Jack said. His tone was casual, almost as though he hadn't actually given a command that Svetlana had to follow. But he had given an order that had to be obeyed, and everyone in the room knew it.

Jack's glass was on the table. Svetlana eased between him and Nigel for it, and when she did, her breasts rubbed lightly against Jack's biceps. Though the contact was fleeting, the touch of silk and solid muscle against her nipples was electrifying, and Svetlana almost allowed a sultry moan to escape her lips. Every nerve in her body was now vibrantly awake, and ready for whatever was about to happen next.

Svetlana made the drink and got the beers. Before returning to the men, she looked down at her breasts. The thin silk somehow made their erect state even more obvious.

I've got the most sensitive nipples in all the world. I must.

She wasn't at all certain whether that was a blessing or a curse.

She resumed her position behind Jack after she had distributed the drinks. Jack resumed talking, discussing options the men might take to fulfill the mission. As he spoke, Svetlana placed her hand lightly on his broad shoulder, touching him through his cotton suit coat and shirt.

Almost immediately Jack stopped talking, and when he did, Svetlana knew that she had made a mistake that she would now pay for. She could only wonder what the punishment was for her transgressing.

Jack pushed his chair away from the table and rose to his feet. Suddenly, to Svetlana, he seemed very large, almost a giant though her heels added five inches to her height.

"You like to get handsy, don't you?"

Svetlana had no idea what the right response should be.

"Turn around," Jack said, his tone of voice authoritarian. When Svetlana turned her back to him, he said, "Put your wrists together. One on top of the other behind your back."

Svetlana felt her nipples get just a little bit tighter, more sensitive, when she realized he was going to tie her wrists.

How does he know what I like? She knew the answer. *He does because he's just like Burke.*

She put her hands behind her back and felt a silk necktie being wrapped around them and knotted tightly. He wasn't gentle.

"That should keep you from being handsy for the rest of this meeting," Jack said, pleasure in his tone. "But with someone like you, it seems to me that more than one necktie will be necessary."

Svetlana gasped softly. She didn't know what that meant, and there was nothing more frightening to her than the unknown.

She heard Nigel say, "Here you go, mate."

"Good man," Jack replied.

A moment later the necktie was used as a blindfold. With her heartrate and breathing rapidly escalating, Svetlana found herself standing in a luxury hotel room blindfolded and with her hands tied behind her back, with three men she had only met earlier in the day.

"Now let's get back to the aerial photos of the compound," she heard Jack say. "Maybe we've overlooked something."

You're not just going to leave me standing here blindfolded and tied up, are you? You can't be that cruel.

But Jack was that cruel. For ten long minutes he kept her standing there, sightless and helpless as Jack and the others kicked over possible avenues of action to take. As they did, Svetlana discovered that it was very easy to lose her balance when she couldn't see anything.

There was sudden silence in the room. Svetlana could guess that the men were using hand signals, or something of that nature, to silently communicate with each other.

Their silence was scary.

She heard three chairs get pushed away from the long table. Her vagina clenched at the possibilities of what was about to happen.

Since she could not see, her hearing now seemed profoundly acute. She spread her feet just a little wider apart for better balance.

Not even Burke has ever done anything like this to me.

She could hear footsteps. The men were moving, but it was impossible to tell who was walking where. Svetlana's brain was spinning, and it suddenly occurred to her that she could have made a very serious mistake by agreeing to a mission that by any credible standard would be horribly dangerous, working with three men she had never met and knew almost nothing about.

And then she felt fingertips touch her cheek. The contact of flesh to flesh was gentle, but that didn't stop Svetlana was gasping softly and flinching sharply.

She tried to tell herself that it was just a man touching her cheek, but with her hands bound behind her back and being blindfolded, it seemed so much more intimate than just that. So much more . . . erotic.

"Who . . . who is touching me?"

She expected one of them to say something, perhaps one of them to at least chuckle so that she could figure out which of the three men was caressing her with the gentlest of touches. But none of them said a word. She couldn't even hear them breathe. And that was more than just a little eerie.

"Please," she said softly. She could hear the ache, the longing, and the anxiety in her voice. "Someone say something."

While the fingertips lightly caressed her cheek, a long-fingered hand cupped her left breast through her blouse. Svetlana gasped when her breast was squeezed. Her pussy throbbed with escalating need.

A moment later there were hands all over her body, touching both of her breasts, squeezing them, pinching her nipples through her blouse. Someone moved behind her, and she felt his hands at her hips, then felt his pelvis against her bound hands. She could feel that she had aroused him, though his solid erection was still inside the slacks of his pedestrian suit of clothes.

Please . . . someone kiss me.

Svetlana wanted to scream the words that would confess her passionate needs, but she didn't dare.

And she didn't need to.

The fingers that had been caressing her cheek so gently slipped around to the back of her neck to hold her, and then warm, moist, masculine lips were pressing against hers.

Oh, God . . . I've never tasted such a kiss, and I don't know who is kissing me.

Svetlana parted her lips. It was an invitation to make the kiss even deeper, more personal, and the invitation wasn't ignored. When the man—whoever he was—slipped his tongue between her lips, Svetlana moaned softly, soulfully, and put her tongue in motion against his.

Whoever was standing directly behind her was now moving his hips from side to side, alternately rubbing his hard cock against Svetlana's hands, and then her ass. Every time she got the chance, Svetlana gave the shaft of his cock a squeeze, but since he never stopped moving, she never got to do it for very long at any one time.

Someone grabbed Svetlana by the chin and forcibly turned her face to the side, ending the luscious French kiss that she had been enjoying. An instant later, with the strong hand holding tightly onto her chin, a new mouth was pressed passionately against hers, and a new tongue was dancing with hers.

Oh, God . . . what's happening to me?

As she kissed the new man to her right, the one holding her chin so tightly, the man who had been kissing her mouth turned his passionate attention to Svetlana's throat. He bared his teeth and nipped lightly. While Svetlana French kissed one man, the neck-biter soothed away the discomfort he'd caused by using his tongue warmly, wetly, and most certainly erotically.

The next shocking awareness for Svetlana was that someone was kneeling in front of her, and was very slowly pushing his palms up her legs, staring at her knees.

Who is it? I want to know who it is.

But the men were as silent as ghosts as they electrified every nerve in her body.

The man to her right who had been kissing her mouth stopped. And then, suddenly and disastrously, all three of the men stopped pleasuring her.

Oh, God . . . have I done something wrong?

The thought of them stopping their seduction now was something too cruel for Svetlana to contemplate. It zipped through her mind that she had serious money in two different, secret bank accounts, totaling several million dollars that had been taken from drug dealers and illegal weapons merchants. Then men in the room with her, in their department store suits, obviously didn't have a lot of money. Would it be possible to bribe them into continuing what they had started? They were mercenaries, after all. Surely, they could be bought . . . couldn't they?

Thoughts of bribery vanished when she heard the men walking, moving in a circle around her. She realized that even though she didn't know who was who, they were protecting their identity by changing positions.

Or maybe they just wanted access to a different part of her body.

It was clear to Svetlana that this wasn't the first time these three men had played this game with a woman, and — acidly — she resented the hell out of whatever women these men had bestowed their delightful skills upon in the past.

Someone was now standing directly in front of her. He had strong hands, and he was squeezing her breasts firmly without being a brute about it. Then Svetlana felt him ease his fingers into her blouse between the buttons. His hands clenched into tight fists.

An instant later the fists rocketed apart, and the buttons gave way to much greater strength. She gasped loudly as her blouse was ripped open, exposing her naked breasts.

It was sinfully arousing to not know who had just violated her clothing with such brutal force.

Whoever had ripped open her blouse was sucking hungrily, lustily upon her nipples seconds later.

"Fuck," Svetlana whispered, thinking once again that her nipples simply *had* to be more responsive than those of other women.

Strong hands were moving up the insides of her legs, starting at the knees and gliding up to her inner thighs. That meant that one of the three men had to be on his knees, while the one giving her nipples such lusty oral attention had to be standing directly behind him, bending over so that he could reach her breasts.

"I can hardly breathe," Svetlana heard herself say. She hadn't really intended on saying anything. The words just sort of came out of her mouth without her summoning them. "That's not true. I'm breathing so fast I'm going to hyperventilate."

The hands that had been caressing her thighs pushed up beneath her miniskirt, then curled into the waistband of her panties.

He's going to go down on me.

She didn't know how she should feel about that. A huge

portion of her better judgment was screaming in her brain that she had let this whole crazy, lusty encounter go much farther into the realm of sexual adventuring than she had ever thought it would. Sex with the gangsters meant she was fulfilling the requirements of the mission. Getting joyously gangbanged by three mercenaries she had just met, and who were providing the muscle of the mission, could not even remotely be excused as a chore she was duty-bound to satisfy.

As her panties were being slowly brought down her legs, Svetlana felt two things simultaneously — two things that she had never before felt at exactly the same time.

She felt the lips of one man kiss her pelvis, very near her cunt. And she felt the lips of another man kiss the right cheek of her ass, very near her back entrance. She had men kneeling in front of her and behind her.

Oh, God . . . they're not going to . . . at the same time . . . are they?

She wondered if she could even maintain her balance if she got rimmed by one man while she got her pussy magnificently licked by another.

She was able to remain standing, but only because there were very strong, commanding hands holding her by the hips. Otherwise, she most assuredly would have fallen to the floor.

Svetlana had never experienced anything quite like this. Her hands were bound behind her back, triggering her fetish for bondage. She was blindfolded, causing her to experience a whole new area of her libido that had heretofore been either ignored or undiscovered. She had a skilled tongue delving between the lips of her cunt and paying rather careful attention to her clit. She had a tongue toying with her ass, tickling nerve endings that seldom felt an oral caress. And she had a warm, wet mouth that was moving from one breast to the other, sucking on nipples that were engorged and more sensitive than a safecracker's fingertips.

Svetlana didn't just climax, she exploded. Almost literally.

She was screaming. As the convulsive waves of ecstasy pounded through her body, Svetlana was consciously aware of the fact that she was screaming, and that she probably shouldn't. Even though she was in the penthouse suite, the soundproofing could only muffle so much.

At that point, good judgment didn't really matter. Neither did the possibility that the hotel's management might not be so thrilled about having a hysterical resident in the penthouse suite. All that mattered to Svetlana was that *she* was thrilled — beyond words, and that was why she was screaming loudly and incoherently.

And then, when the convulsive, climactic spasms ended, her entire body, which had been so receptive to everything the men were doing to her, was suddenly *way* to sensitive to allow even one more second of stimulation.

"Stop! Fucking stop! Stop or I'll kill you!"

The men did, but afterward, she wished that they would have kept a tighter hold on her. The instant they let go of Svetlana, she fell rather heavily onto her knees, hitting the carpeted floor with a grunt that was forced from her lungs.

With her hands still tied behind her back and her body suddenly housing muscles that simply had no strength left in them, Svetlana slumped to the side, and would have hit the floor if someone — she still didn't have any idea of which man was doing what to her — hadn't caught her, and then rather gently laid her on her side.

"Let me rest for a moment," Svetlana said, her voice muffled. She was exhausted. "That . . . that couldn't have been natural."

CHAPTER THREE

"What do we know about the Venezuelan deal?" Rico asked his younger brother. "Do you think we can trust them?"

"Let me answer those questions in reverse order," Tomas replied. He smiled. "Can we trust them? Hell, no. Can we trust anyone? Hell, no. But what we do know is that they've made promises of nearly a half ton of cocaine to their distributors, and the last three shipments coming to them from other suppliers have been taken by either the Mexican navy, or the American Coast Guard. Their distributors are getting angry and impatient. That means if we fill in for the shipments that have been confiscated, we can legitimately charge more per ton." Tomas made a motion with his hands. "Yes, some will say that we're price gouging — which we are — but we'll counter by saying that our costs have gone up because of increased law enforcement presence. They won't like to hear that, but so what? They need what we've got, and that means we've got them by the balls."

Rico smiled and closed his eyes, turning his chair toward the large bank of windows at his back. He was enormously impressed with his younger brother, who seemed to be learning more about the family business — not with each passing week, but with each passing day. He had gone from being the kid brother he had to have in the business to the young up-and-comer that he wanted at his side, irrespective of the fact that they were siblings.

"When do you think we can close the deal?" Rico asked.

"I've been talking with their negotiator, and he thinks that the day after tomorrow would be perfect for them. There are a few details we've got to work out," Tomas answered, "but there is nothing that comes even close to being a deal-breaker."

"Nice job. Very, very well done," Rico said, leaning back in the thickly upholstered leather chair in his office. "Now what do you have in mind?"

"I'm glad you asked," Tomas replied, smiling broadly, "because even though we've been unable to find a girl who interests both of us enough to invite her to stay for a week or so, I have touched base with someone we both know—and have enjoyed immensely." He got up out of his chair, then knocked on the office door from inside the room. A moment later Rico heard knuckles on the opposite side of the door, and the giggle of a young woman.

"What did you pay her?" Rico asked. One-timers were sometimes expensive. Rico was wealthy, but it hadn't always been that way.

"Not as much as she's worth, and most of the payment was in cocaine."

"You always have been a good negotiator," Rico said, genuinely impressed with his brother's business acumen.

Tomas opened the office door, and Rico looked at the young woman standing at the threshold, waiting for an invitation to enter.

Rico couldn't remember if the girl was eighteen or nineteen. One or the other. It didn't really matter, so long as she wasn't underage. Tomas had found her in some little village miles from Mexico City, working—of all things—at a gas station that doubled as the village's grocery store. She had been making something less than nothing a week. The only thing she had going for her was a trim, compact body, a complexion that was that delicious almond color, and a smile that had enough voltage in it to light up the dusty, dirt-road village she lived in.

She had stayed at the compound nearly three weeks, which was a record that had not been matched since. The only real reason Rico had made her leave the compound was because she had become just a little too comfortable with her living arrangements, and had assumed just *way* too much about how badly Rico and Tomas needed her. Therefore, she got the heave-ho, but not before she received a severance package, putting in her pocket at one time more than her family and the rest of the village could make in half a year.

The girl was wearing a white strap-sleeved T-shirt that was several sizes too small for her. It looked like a child's T-shirt, and it had been cropped to not just show off her midriff, which was flat and lovely to look at, but also the undercurve of her breasts, which were gently rounded, and also lovely to look at. Beneath that she wore a simple white cotton pair of thong panties.

They didn't quite match the crop-top T-shirt, but Rico still gave her credit for trying.

He was always impressed — or at least *pleased* — when the hired help made an effort.

But what was her name? Rico could remember a thousand things about her, but not her name.

"Señor Santiago, may I not come in?"

Her voice was soft, very timid, and Rico could hear the uncertainty that was bubbling in her soul.

"Of course, little bambino," Rico said, giving her a smile and turning his face slightly so that she could see his best profile. "It is so good to see you again. We've missed you."

Tomas said quickly, "But just for tonight. Then you've got to leave."

Rico saw the words register in the girl's consciousness. She wanted more money than just what one night would bring.

All of the girls did, but with this one—whatever the hell her name was—Rico was actually considering it.

"My brother and I still have some business to discuss," Rico said, leaning back in his desk chair, "so why don't you pour us some tequila, and then make yourself useful."

Rico watched as she hurried about her business, taking the bottle of Mexican tequila from the freezer and pouring two small glasses of it, then hurrying to serve them. The T-shirt was very tight and so thin that he could see the dark circles of her areolas through it. Her stomach was flat, and he thought she had a very cute navel, which he would have paid to have pierced had she been more important to him.

After she'd served him his tequila, she served Tomas his, then she turned and started around the desk once again.

"No. First my brother. He's been doing such excellent work lately, he deserves to be at the head of the line," Rico said, double entendre intended.

The girl stopped quickly, and looked into Rico's eyes for confirmation.

"Yes. Please. My brother first. Hurry up now. Don't leave him waiting. You know how impatient he can be." Rico took a sip of his ice-cold tequila. It was the first sip of the evening, and that was always the best one. Everything after that was going downhill.

He watched as the girl turned and walked to his brother. In her thong panties, he saw that she had a gorgeous ass, and even though he had scored with more women than he could possibly count and most certainly could remember, he had bleary, vague memories of being pleased with her ass. And with her demeanor in general. She had always seemed quite pleased to be at the compound. There were others who in their attitude made it quite clear to Rico that they were only there for the financial payout at the end of the week.

Those girls never lasted more than a week, and the instant

Rico realized that they were only there for the money, he turned on the rough stuff, and he didn't stop giving it to them hard and mean until one of his soldiers put them in a cab and sent them back to Mexico City, or whatever impoverished village they came from.

He watched as his younger brother, like a young prince being given his royal privilege by a maid, leaned back in the overstuffed chair that faced Rico's desk and kicked his legs out.

The girl, with a small giggle, sank to her knees between his and began unbuckling his belt without hesitation.

"Now where were we?" Rico asked. Whatever they were going to talk about had to be inconsequential, since they tried to not talk business in front of transitory hired help.

"The contractor for the outdoor hot tub," Tomas said, his tone remarkably calm, considering the fact that an attractive young woman had just opened his trousers, taking his cock out through the fly of his boxer underwear, and was planting light, smacking, audible kisses on the head of his cock. "Every time I talk to him, he always says that there has been some kind of complication that he hasn't anticipated." He closed his eyes for a moment. "Oh, fuck, that feels good."

"How much have we paid him so far?"

Tomas gave him the total in Mexican pesos and American dollars.

"Do you think we should stick with him, or look for another contractor?"

Tomas chuckled softly. Rico watched as his kid brother stroked the girl's hair while she sucked on his cock, which was now rock-solid.

"Well?" Rico prodded. This was part of the game they played, pretending to not be affected while getting a blow job.

"I'd say we stick with the one we've got, but I'll let him know that he's not going to blackmail us into giving him any more money than the original estimate."

Tomas bent forward at the waist and squeezed the girl's nipple through the T-shirt, then pulled the garment up to get at her small, naked breast.

Señorita . . . Damn it, what was her name? Rico wasn't displeased with himself that he couldn't remember the girl's name. Once he was finished with a sexual partner, they were about as relevant to him as a complete stranger that he'd never met.

He watched as the girl's lips moved slowly up and down over the shaft of Tomas's cock, and he felt his own penis take notice, twitching a little, awakening, slowly but steadily thickening and lengthening.

He tried to take a sip of his tequila, but discovered that he'd finished the small glass. This would make for a nice opportunity to mess with his brother.

"Señorita, my princess, will you please get me another?"

Rico noticed that Tomas wasn't at all happy that his blow job was being put on hold, but they both knew that interruptions were part of the game they played.

Without a hint of embarrassment, the girl rose to her feet, went to the desk to retrieve Rico's glass, then went to the bar. When Rico looked into his brother's eyes, he saw the annoyance that Tomas was shrewd enough to keep to himself.

"Don't worry," Rico said, humor in his tone, "she'll be back soon enough."

Tomas raised his glass toward Rico in a silent toast, grinned, then finished his own tequila.

It was a good-natured game that the brothers played, and they both enjoyed it.

Someone had helped Svetlana get up onto her knees. She didn't know which of the three men had done it. Her body was still tingling, her skin still hyper-sensitive from the shockingly intense orgasm the men had given her.

She felt a little guilty for having climaxed with them. She had thought she had better self-control than that . . . but with three tongues—clearly highly-talented, very experienced tongues—tickling and caressing her in the most erotic ways imaginable, what choice did she have but to climax?

It wasn't my fault. There's three of them, and only one of me.

It was a self-serving justification, and she knew it. But what she didn't know was how Jack had so completely divined the truth about her submissive fetish. How had he figured out her sexual weakness in a shockingly short period of time?

Only rare men can do something like that.

Her chin was on her chest, and she was quickly regaining her senses, her ability to think clearly and logically coming back to her.

One thing that logic told her was that though she had just experienced a climax for the ages—but the men hadn't. Not even one of them. And the odds were less than zero that they'd let her go without her providing climaxes they felt were commensurate in power and scope with the one they had given her.

She had known enough powerful men of action to understand that they wouldn't meekly ride off into the sunset with a pair of blue balls between their legs. Men like that didn't put up with cockteasers.

Someone put a hand on her shoulder and pushed just enough to get her to be a little straighter while she remained on her knees. Someone else reached down and tenderly rubbed his palm over her erect left nipple before giving the breast a gentle squeeze.

Someone else ran the tip of his finger back and forth over her mouth, first over the top lip, and then over the bottom. Then the finger moved to the center of her mouth and gently but insistently pushed forward, separating her lips.

I should resist.

It was a silly, foolish, prideful thought, and she knew it. Svetlana opened her mouth just a little. The finger eased portentously into her mouth. She tightened her lips around the finger as it moved deeper into her mouth. She caressed the digit with her tongue, and the act she was pantomiming simply could not be misinterpreted.

The finger moved back and forth between her lips, and Svetlana moaned softly.

They're going to make me suck their cocks. I'll have to do what they make me do.

Another self-justification. If they didn't make her give them blow jobs, she would complain vociferously, probably using a great deal of profanity. And there was crass bribery that she could fall back on, if all else failed.

The finger was removed from her mouth. Svetlana resisted the urge to moan disapprovingly or speak of her disappointment.

Then she felt the spongy crown of a cock touch her lips, and she realized that her fears were without foundation.

These men are a long, long way from being finished with me.

The thought didn't displease her in the least.

For several seconds she wondered whether she would turn them on more by resisting their wishes, or if they'd like it if she very willing opened her lips wide to let them know her body was there for the taking. The warm, manly flesh pressed more insistently against her lips. Svetlana, being unable to decide which was the most erotic approach to take, took half-measures, and opened her mouth just a little.

The cockhead forced it open a lot more than that, and a moment later she had an erection flattening her tongue to the bottom of her mouth and rubbing against the roof. She immediately tightened her lips around the shaft of the cock once the head had moved completely past her lips.

She heard a low, masculine groan of approval, but she

didn't have enough experience with the men she was with to be able to tell who had groaned.

I'm on my knees, giving a blow job . . . and I don't know which man is in my mouth.

That was a surreal reality for Svetlana to wrap her brain around. She tested the necktie around her wrists to see if she might somehow escape, then realized with cringing embarrassment that she already knew she couldn't—besides, she was right where she wanted to be.

The cock had made three or four passing motions between her lips when Svetlana realized that she was, quite possibly, the luckiest secret agent the world had ever known, or *not* known. While a mouth-filling cock glided between her lips, warm, manly lips were suddenly sucking on her breasts. Not just one nipple. No. No. She had hot, wet mouths sucking on both of her nipples at the same time.

It's the blindfold that's messing up all my perceptions. I don't know who is doing what to me. I hate not knowing.

But she knew that wasn't true. It was the not-knowing part that was actually arousing her to the marrow of her bones, to the core of her soul.

Whoever was standing in front of her and feeding her his cock put his hands lightly atop her head. Svetlana at first expected him to either start pulling her hair, or begin to forcefully, maybe even brutally, face-fuck her.

Nothing of the sort happened. The cock pushed into her mouth until the crown was pressing snuggly against the opening of her throat, but it wasn't like he was driving hard and fast, causing her to gag.

Then, just when Svetlana was getting into the ebb and flow rhythm of motion of the man, he pulled completely out of her mouth.

Once again, Svetlana had to stifle a moan of dissatisfaction. This was a game showing more promise with each passing second. But sometimes it could be vexing.

She wasn't in the doldrums long. Whoever had been sucking on her right nipple stopped, and Svetlana heard the movement of the men again. They circled around her several times, and Svetlana understood that this was to confuse her, just in case they had somehow let their identity known.

New lips were on her nipples, and a new cock was in her mouth. Svetlana's pussy was as wet as she could ever remember, even though it wasn't being touched, caressed, or anything even remotely resembling either of those two things.

Can they actually make me come without touching my pussy?

Now *that* was an interesting question to ponder. She accepted that her nipples were very sensitive, but still . . . .

But she didn't have to ponder it for long. Cock Number Two apparently had used up his allotted time, and he pulled his delicious erection out of her mouth, only to be instantly replaced by Cock Number Three, who, Svetlana noted with no small measure of approval, tasted just as delicious and was just as satisfying to suck on as the two cocks that preceded it. Once again, Svetlana found herself getting slowly and delightfully face-fucked, while two men sucked on her nipples . . . but this time one of the men reached between her wide-spread thighs and began slipping first one, and then two, fingers in and out of her pussy while rubbing her clit with the most subtle of touches.

Thirty seconds later, Svetlana twisted her head sharply on her shoulders to get the cock out of her mouth, and like before, her banshee scream was loud enough throughout her orgasm to wake the dead.

CHAPTER FOUR

The last of the tremors had gone through Tomas. He made a point of not looking at his brother, who was sitting behind his desk. He wasn't sure what he'd see in Rico's eyes. Tomas wondered if he'd lasted long enough without climaxing, or if Rico would think that he'd come too quickly.

There was only one man in the world who could make Tomas feel insecure, and it was his older brother. Rico was the only person whose approval Tomas valued at all. It had always been that way, even from the very beginning.

"That's enough now," Tomas said. The girl had continued nursing on his cock for a full thirty second after he had finished his orgasm.

He watched as she tilted her head back on her shoulders, allowing his dwindling cock to slide out from between her lips. She smiled kittenishly, and in her eyes was a look of triumph. Tomas felt drained, and defeated somehow.

"Let me make your brother happy," she said in a very soft voice. "Then, if you want me again, you can have me again. Okay?"

"Okay." But he wasn't sure he wanted her again. It seemed they had gone to battle and she had won.

Tomas watched as she rose to her feet, her movements lithe and fluid, then walked around his brother's desk as he swiveled his chair to face her. She sank to her knees without saying a word. The smile on her face was angelic. A fallen angel, perhaps, but an angel nevertheless.

Later tonight, we'll DP the bitch. But she's only staying one night, and then she's out of here.

The last thing in the world that Tomas needed was for a woman to think she had some possession over him and Rico. Neither Rico nor Tomas were going to let that happen.

Svetlana felt strong hands grab her by the upper arms, then forcibly haul her to her feet. She only had one shoe on, so she was wobbly.

"Can you please take my shoe off, or put the other one back on? I can't believe I'm wearing only one shoe."

She expected one of them to answer, but none of the men said a word or made so much as a single sound.

They are taking the strong, silent type stuff way too far.

The hands at her biceps changed. A new man now held her. They were going to make it impossible to guess which of them was doing what to her. Svetlana was more convinced than ever that she wasn't the first woman they had introduced to this experience. Their movements were too choreographed.

She could hear that someone was getting onto the bed. The hands surrounding her biceps were holding her tightly. They turned her around so that she faced the bed, then lifted her. She raised a knee up onto the mattress and felt a thickly muscled, naked thigh brushing against hers as she got up onto the bed. A moment later she found herself on her knees, straddling a pair of very muscular thighs, while two other men got up onto the bed without ever releasing their hold on her arms.

"You're going to fuck me, aren't you?" A moment later she laughed in a short, self-deprecating manner. "Of course you're going to fuck me. What was I thinking?"

The hands that held her moved her into position. Svetlana soon felt the crown of a plump cock pressing against the entrance to her sex, and she wondered which of the trio was going to fuck her first. She suspected it would be Jack. He was the Alpha, after all, so he'd take her first. Svetlana understood this instinctively, as a true-borne submissive would. Nigel and Brad were manly, to be sure, but they followed Jack's orders. The power dynamics weren't equal.

The man was on his back, and his hands — long-fingered and strong — grasped her by the hips, holding her in place. The head of his cock was again the lips of Svetlana's sex, but he neither pulled her down to impale her nor pushed up into her.

As with virtually everything else they'd done to Svetlana, their actions confused her. The only thing that didn't disorient her was her own certainty that these men were going to fuck her however the hell they wanted to, and there really wasn't anything Svetlana could do to change that immutable fact, one way or another.

She was helpless against them, she trusted them completely, and her pussy was getting wetter with each passing moment.

The seconds stretched on. When Svetlana could take no more suspense, she said softly, "Please, don't torment me. Fuck or set me free. I can't — "

The protest died when the hands at her hips tightened and then pulled her down, forcing his rounded cockhead to separate the lips of her cunt. When Svetlana's body stretched to accommodate, her mouth opened wide in a silent gasp of shock and splendor, and she was immediately aware of the fact that yet another orgasm was building inside her body, and it was only waiting for enough stimulation provided by these three men for that runaway train to reach the station.

Without the use of her hands, it took some getting used to for Svetlana to get her knees properly positioned beneath her so that she could bounce on whoever was beneath her. She might not have known the identity of the man, but she did know that he had a beautiful cock. It was long and thick, and it filled her completely. Her pussy had all it needed.

She had raised and lowered her hips half a dozen times before firm hands surrounded her face, then turned her head on her shoulders. A moment later, when Svetlana felt the crown of a man's cock touching her mouth, she didn't even pretend to put forth any resistance. She opened her lips and tasted the cock of a man whose identity she did not know.

Don't dwell on that too much.

She was pleased with herself that there was still a part of her brain that was logical.

The reality was that she had a cock in her pussy and another one in her mouth, and she didn't know who belonged to either one of them. It was a fact that was very difficult for her to come to terms with.

But those cocks *did* excite her. More than she had thought possible.

With firm guidance from the man beneath her, Svetlana raised and lowered her hips, her excitement mounting each time she dropped down onto the man's torso and his cock was thrust as deeply inside her that she could feel it in her soul.

He had firm, strong hands, and he guided her movements with determination. He seemed frighteningly strong, and that made the honey ooze to her pussy. Dominating masculine strength almost always affected her that way.

The man who was fucking her mouth had his hands tight on either side of Svetlana's head. He was churning his hips steadily but slowly. He was clearly in no hurry to reach the peak of the mountain. Svetlana was pleased with that. She was in the mood for a marathon, not a sprint to the finish.

Then there were strong hands on her shoulders. The man was on his knees behind her. He pushed down, forcing Svetlana to take the cock full-length into her pussy, and the other cock out of her mouth. Her mind was in a whirl. She clenched her hands into fists. Irreversible decisions were being made about what was going to be done to her, and no one was asking for her opinion.

Svetlana felt her breasts touch the man's chest. Her nipples were hard and achingly sensitive, and she was instantly aware of both the heat of his body, and of the muscles in his chest. To press against him was to feel what amounted to masculine perfection. It was nothing less than that.

Who is it?

It was an impossible question. All three of the mercenaries were as fit as professional soccer players. Not a one of them had an ounce of flab. They were the height of masculinity.

They can probably fuck for days.

She suspected this was true. She wasn't at all certain how she felt about that. Her emotions were in tumult.

It was certainly not a thought that brought with it comfort and tranquility for Svetlana.

With her body pressed against the man beneath her, the next sensation that Svetlana was shockingly aware of was a finger, slick with an intimate lubricating ointment, moving slowly over her taboo entrance.

Somebody wants my ass.

She was about to say something, but the man beneath her — the one whose cock filled her pussy so completely and delightfully — put his hands on her face to turn her toward him sharply, and then he kissed her fiercely, hotly. It was a kiss that demanded a response — and Svetlana's body did. Her cunt creamed, and the climax that had seemed quite far off just moments earlier now seemed to be approaching significantly faster.

The finger at her ass smoothed the lube liberally around her tight opening, then began to delicately probe. Svetlana shivered. It was arousing to have the back door tantalized while she kissed a handsome man whose erection currently filled her pussy so completely that she could not want for anything more without establishing herself to be an incredibly selfish woman.

She tried to relax her muscles, found she couldn't, then

discovered it didn't matter. The finger pushed past her resistance, past the ring of muscle at her back entrance, and was then inside her.

She was no novice to going Greek, but it was something special — a taboo thrill — that she seldom indulged in. She always loved it when Burke took her that way — and he was the only man to ever do so — but she always felt a little guilty, as though she had taken profound pleasure in something that she shouldn't have. She always felt naughty afterward.

She also knew that naughty pleasures were always the most satisfying.

The finger moved back and forth, all the way into her ass, until she could feel the man's palm against the cheeks of her bottom, then withdrawing all the way out to caress the entrance with smooth, artful circles that set Svetlana's blood boiling.

Svetlana sucked on the tongue that was in her mouth. He was holding her face tightly and kissing her demandingly, and it was everything that Svetlana could ever want in a kiss. She just didn't know which of three men it was.

How fucking erotic is that?

The blindfold was still in place, but there was enough loose hair for the man who had been feeding her his cock to grab her by the hair and raise her face. Svetlana felt the strands of her hair tug against her scalp, and the discomfort this caused made her pussy clench around the cock that filled it. Every sensation, whether or pain or pleasure, heightened her passion.

"Ah," she gasped when the man gripping her hair gave her head a little shake. He shook her head a second time in an act of utter domination, and a low groan came from Svetlana's throat. She knew the game he was playing. She was playing it, too. And it turned her on.

After that, she couldn't say anything because there was a large hard cock filling her mouth.

Experience had taught Svetlana that large cocks stifled co-herent speech. At least it did with her.

The finger was removed from her bottom, and just seconds later, Svetlana felt a heavy, powerful chest against her back at the same time she felt the crest of a man's cock nudging against her taboo entrance.

Airtight. They're going to make me airtight.

A high-pitched sound of alarm came from deep within Svetlana's throat as two cocks made slow, relentless invasions into her body, immediately followed by retreats. Beneath her, the man fucking her pussy was doing it slowly, but with de-termination. With Svetlana's face turned to the side, the sec-ond man was filling her mouth with his arousal, not stopping until his knob was pressed against the back of Svetlana's mouth and threatening to drive down her throat. And above her, most vividly of all, she could feel the pounding heartbeat of the man who was putting greater and greater pressure against her ass. He wanted entrance, and Svetlana suspected he was a man who was successful in whatever he set out to do.

Once again, she tried to relax, but she couldn't. Her re-sistance didn't matter. Significantly greater masculine strength overpowered feminine reluctance, and Svetlana's body opened to accept hard, determined flesh. She whim-pered softly for a moment as twinges of discomfort went through her — this was not her usual method of accepting men into her body — but after only a couple seconds, she felt noth-ing other than that unique sensation of having a cock moving back and forth between her buns. The feel was *so* different from anything else in the sexual realm. Different . . . and a lit-tle scary . . . and a lot exciting.

They know what they're doing. They know how this is supposed to be done to please a woman. Lucky me. Lucky fucking me.

It was a blissful awareness for Svetlana. If her trio of lovers hadn't understood all the unwritten rules in triple-penetrating a woman, it could have been very painful and most definitely nothing near ecstasy. But they did know, taking their time at first, letting her willing and accommodating body adjust to all the changes it had to make to take the ecstasy that they offered.

They weren't good. They were *fucking fantastic*.

Svetlana wondered if she'd ever tell them that.

Around the hard arousal that filled her mouth, thirty seconds after she'd experienced the forbidden thrill of having three men into her body at the same time, Svetlana moaned softly. It was a wordless signal to let the men know that she could take everything they had to give. It was the kind of invitation those types of men lived for, and they responded accordingly.

Hardly had she moaned before the men increased their tempo, the rhythm of their torsos not suddenly kicking into high gear, but certainly moving with a bit more determination than previously, a bit more urgency. Svetlana didn't have to change a thing. She was the receptacle of their passion, the central focus of all their sexual energies, and all she had to do was be there . . . and enjoy.

Oh, God, they're going to make me come again.

Svetlana squeezed her eyes tightly shut beneath the blindfold and told herself that no matter what, she mustn't let her teeth scrape against the cock that was seesawing between her lips. Very bad form to get face-fucked, then let teeth become a part of the man's experience.

Almost there. Oh, fuck, I'm almost there.

She felt the powerful body above her crushing her hands to the small of her back as he thrust full-length into her bottom. His pelvis was like a V-8 engine, fine-tuned and racing full-out. He was burning high-octane and revving accordingly.

I've got so much cock inside me.

It was a lurid thought to have when another orgasm was

just seconds away. It occurred to her that maybe she should be ashamed of herself. But she wasn't. Not even a little.

Her clit felt as tight and aroused as it ever had been in her life. The man beneath her, the one filling her sex with hard, unrelenting masculinity, was writhing beneath her, trapped under the weight of her body as well as that of whoever was above her. She could feel him strain to drive his cock into her deeper, farther, then withdraw for an instant before repeating the process. He was struggling, and his massive effort aroused everything feminine in Svetlana.

There was one man on his knees near her shoulder, and he was holding her head with both hands, and he was fucking her mouth with ever-increasing intensity. She could hear his labored breathing, and she could tell that he couldn't last much longer.

So . . . much . . . cock.

It was a delirious reality that her mind could hardly comprehend.

Oh, fuck. It's going to happen . . . now!

It wasn't a gentle experience to climax with three big, virile men thrashing inside her body. To have an orgasm with three cocks of significant length and girth pistoning in and out of every orifice she possessed capable of accepting an erection was mind-boggling, surreal. Her pussy tightened, flexing around the manliness that filled it. So did her ass. Strange, only vaguely human sounds came from Svetlana as a tsunami of intense emotions washed over her, buffeting her against the rocky shore of sensuality with a brutal intensity that was as sexually draining as it was violent. Svetlana had never experienced anything like it.

Somewhere during the tumult of her climax, two of the men climaxed. She felt the man beneath her relax after she heard him groan, and only seconds later, the man above her slumped over her back, his body almost bruising her hands, which were bound and trapped between their bodies. Her bottom ached in a most delightful way. She was sandwiched between them, and their bodies were very warm.

She was only barely sentient when the third man—the one fucking her mouth—reached the summit of ecstasy. His sperm gushed from him in a great torrent, and Svetlana, who normally would have been able to accept such things, choked on the eruption. She leaned to the side so that the cum, spilling out of her mouth because she couldn't swallow it, wouldn't fall on the man beneath her. She coughed several times. This was not the post-orgasmic lassitude for herself that she had hoped for.

My God, he comes a lot.

It was not a taste that she appreciated.

She hoped she hadn't disappointed anyone. Svetlana felt as though she had just been through a marathon endurance obstacle course, like she had gone through at bootcamp. She had reached the finish line, but she was battered and bruised, exhausted, desperately needing a shower. And to add to the emotional mix, she had no idea who had just done what wickedly sexual things to her.

This isn't the last time they're going to do that to me.

The thought pleased her, and with her cheek against the shoulder of the man beneath her, she smiled from a combination of exhaustion and satisfaction.

What the hell have I just done?

Chapter Five

The shower had been scalding hot, but that was the way Svetlana had wanted it. When she stepped out of the shower and looked at herself in the bathroom mirror, her pale skin was pink in most places, and almost red in others.

They're going to do that to me again.

The thought came to Svetlana without fear. The awareness that they were going to triple penetrate her again was something that made her shiver with anticipation. The orgasm she'd experienced when she had a man in her pussy, in her bottom, and in her mouth — and all at the same time — was orgasm that she would never forget. It was one of such spine-wrenching physicality that she doubted anything in the future could favorably compare to what she had just experienced.

Don't be silly. If they made it happen once, they can make it happen again.

Svetlana looked at her clean, naked body in the bathroom mirror, and for a moment wondered if she would ever again be truly clean.

Of course you'll be clean. But you won't be the same. Once three men have made you airtight, every other sexual situation is something else . . . something less than being airtight. Not necessarily something bad . . . but not airtight. It takes three men to do that.

The thought sent a shiver ripple up her spine.

Are they going to want me again . . . tonight?

It was an uneasy possibility for Svetlana to consider.

Do I want them again?

She knew the answer to that. Yes, of course she did. She wasn't at all certain what she would eventually tell Burke about her sexual activity, but she knew with absolute certainty that she wanted Jack, Nigel, and Brad again . . . she wanted them physically, and she wanted them sexually unleashed so that their virile energy could be thoroughly and completely set free. She couldn't put the genie back in the bottle, even if she wanted to.

The thought made Svetlana tremble and squeeze her eyes tightly shut. She hadn't meant for it to register in her consciousness, but it had.

Makeup first. Never let them see you without makeup. In Svetlana's life, that was a commandment.

Svetlana smiled at herself in the mirror. Yes, she was thinking clearly now. First, get her face fashion-runway presentable. And after that, there would be a natural progression of events.

But first makeup. Whatever happened after that happened after that. But first makeup, no matter what.

Svetlana blow-dried her hair, then she set about doing her makeup, starting with putting on long eyelashes that would have made a doe envious, then the foundation, eye shadow, touch up on her cheeks, and lastly, the red lipstick that made such a vivid statement. When she was finished, she stood naked in front of the bathroom mirror.

This is as good as I can look.

I sure as hell hope it's good enough.

There were times when her insecurities slowly ate at the structure of her soul, like a termite does to a house. She fought against those times, and mostly she won . . . but sometimes she didn't.

"As near as I can tell, the only place they're vulnerable is when they're on this road here," Jack said, putting his finger on the monitor, where an aerial photo was on the screen. "Somehow, we've got to make them believe that they want to meet her, and not the other way around. If she approaches them, all their paranoid instincts will come to the fore."

"What about the scam we used in Beirut?" Brad asked. "Who can resist a damsel in distress?"

Jack felt a chill go through him. "You know, that worked like a charm in Beirut, and I'll bet it'll work in Mexico City."

"They're bastards," Nigel said, referring to Rico and his men, "but I'll bet they'll stop those SUVs if they see Svetlana in revealing clothing and needing a ride to the nearest service station. But she's got to look like an heiress."

It was at that moment that Svetlana stepped out of the bathroom, and when she did, Jack felt his heart suddenly stop beating. Svetlana was wearing a towel that had been tightly wrapped around her to conceal her from her underarms to the middle of her thighs. She had appropriately covered herself, but there was no doubt that with just a slight tug on the terry cloth towel, she would be completely naked.

"Hi," Svetlana said. "I'm really hoping that someone had the good sense to make some vodka martinis." She laughed softly. "One is not going to be enough."

"Actually, none of us had that good sense," Jack said. "But rest assured, my dear, that the situation will be remedied immediately, and that omission will not be repeated. Attribute it to too much time in all-male company."

Svetlana sat in the single chair near the desk and crossed her legs at the knee. She felt distinctly wanton and wicked wearing only the plush towel, and she liked the feeling. She could sense that the men in the room were looking intently at her, but they were all trying to pretend that they *weren't* paying such careful attention to her.

Deep down in her soul, Svetlana liked the feeling that men such as these were still hungry for her. It did her ego, which could sometimes be fragile, a world of good.

It was nice, she decided, to be lusted after by heroes like these. She knew she should consider herself fortunate.

"Now where are we on the mission?" she asked after Jack had handed her an extra dry vodka martini, garnished with three stuffed olives, precisely the way she liked her cocktails. "Someone get me up to speed. I know you've been talking in my absence, but I'm here now, so let's all work together."

It was an hour later, and Jack had made up his mind. *Brad's idea is what we'll go with.*

Jack wished he'd had the thought himself, but he held no animosity to the man who had come up with a better plan. After all, competence was the reason he kept these men close to him for so many years, wasn't it?

"So when do you think we should set the trap?" Jack asked Brad.

"I'd say as soon as possible," Brad replied. "The clock is ticking."

Jack looked to his left, toward the big sofa not far away. Svetlana was on her back with her legs around Nigel's hips as he pumped into her with both energy and a touch of fury.

Jack understood the emotions, because he had experienced them himself with Svetlana. *He won't last much longer.*

It wasn't a criticism from Jack of Nigel. He knew that Nigel had been making love to Svetlana for quite some time. He suspected that Svetlana had come at least once, and probably twice, during the time Nigel had been dispensing his charms. That elevated his esteem of Nigel. A man should satisfy his partner. There was something lacking in him if he didn't.

Jack felt his own cock begin to reawaken. Even though he had satisfied himself with Svetlana's luscious body earlier in the evening, he found himself wondering just how much pleasure he would experience if he had her on her back one more time that evening. He had learned she was a bottom and liked being on the receiving end of carnal collisions.

He wanted to hear her scream when she climaxed with his cock pounding into her. Her scream was erotic music. Just remembering it brought an expansion to his penis.

He hadn't felt this sexually aroused in years.

Svetlana was bringing out something in him he'd thought was dead and buried, or that he had simply outgrown.

Rico looked at Tomas and asked quietly, in as calm of a voice as he could manage, "So the question is, do we want to make money, or do we want to kill Americans?"

Tomas shrugged his shoulders and leaned back in the comfortable leather office chair he was sitting in. "Frankly, it would be nice to do both, but I understand that we can really only do one of those duties at a time." He took a sip of his cocktail. "I say, first things first, let's make money. Our scientists are working day and night on the new virus. It should poison them by the thousands."

A shiver went through Rico when he thought about killing Americans *by the thousands*. That was almost too much to dream for, too much to pray for. He knew he couldn't single-handedly bring America to its knees, but what a victory it would be to just give that bastard named Uncle Sam a bloody nose.

Rico tried to tell himself that he had to keep his expectations within reason, but the possibility of having tens of thousands of Americans dead and in morgues, their corpses waiting because their bodies were all piled up, waiting to be cremated, was an emotion so joyous it was nearly sexual for him.

He couldn't think of seeing anything more beautiful than

dead American bodies by the thousands.

Rico leaned back in the leather seat of his American-made custom-built SUV limousine and reflected on the day. It hadn't been a good day for Rico, it had been a *spectacular* day. The bank that he and his brother owned thirty-three percent of was doing nicely while laundering not only his own drug money, but that of several of his competitors. Naturally, his competitors didn't know that he was skimming off their deposits, but that made the income so much sweeter. Rico truly loved fucking over anyone dumb enough to trust him. But his bank business wasn't the only enterprise that was running along smoothly and profitably. The construction company he owned sixty-six percent of had just secured a contract with the Mexican government to build several dozen high-rise apartment buildings that were intended to be affordable housing for Mexico City's poor but working population. The cost overruns alone would be worth millions in his pocket, and the legitimate income he'd receive for simply fulfilling the legally binding agreement would be worth many, many millions. The million dollars in American currency he'd given to the south-of-the-border politicians in charge of awarding the contract to make sure that the end result of the bidding would go in his favor would be a magnificent return on investment. The trick in life, he knew, was in bribing the right people.

He inhaled deeply through his nostrils, then exhaled slowly through his mouth. Mexico City had congested traffic and some of the worst air pollution on the planet, but here in his limousine, the air was sweet and clear and clean, and his world was organized exactly as he wanted it to be.

This is almost the exact same model of SUV as the President of the United States has. And I have four of them.

It was a pleasing thought. Especially since he had a limousine outfitted with bullet-proof windows, plus a separate air supply system, should the government or his enemies try to use tear gas or even some kind of nerve gas, on him. The doors had steel plating that could withstand everything but a nuclear bomb. Assault rifles were useless against his method of transportation.

It was, for all practical purposes, a very stylish armored tank.

It also had a small refrigerator that contained cold-cut sandwiches, some ice cream in individual portions, and one-shot plastic bottles of a vast assortment of alcohol. With his telephone and laptop computer, Rico could conduct his worldwide business from the back seat of any of the four limousines and do it as efficiently and comfortably as if he was in his at-home office. And being on the move, it made monitoring him infinitely more difficult, if not impossible, by the authorities.

What more could a self-made billionaire who had just turned forty want?

He looked up and saw a sports car that was stopped in the right lane, perhaps a hundred yards ahead. There was someone standing outside the car — a woman, he could see, though he was too far away to tell much about her — and though he wasn't all that knowledgeable about cars, it seemed to him that the vehicle was an Italian sportster.

That model is about two hundred thousand American dollars.

Rico wasn't impressed by much, but he was impressed by the machine. It took serious money to ride around on four wheels worth just under two hundred thousand dollars.

Rico's interest picked up. Rico figured he could count the number of Lamborghinis in Mexico on the thumbs of his left foot. And what Lamborghinis there were on the streets were all were owned by drug kingpins.

He touched the intercom button on the center console just to his right and said to his driver, "Slow down. Let's see what this is all about."

The chauffeur, who doubled as his bodyguard and occasional assassin, took his foot off the accelerator.

The closer they got, the more clearly Rico could see that the woman was blonde—and in Rico's Latin eyes, that always elevated a woman's beauty—and that she had a shapely figure. She was tall, even remarkably so. And she was wearing a miniskirt that showed off those incredibly long legs in a most delicious way. Rico's interest was mounting with each passing second.

"Much slower," Rico said to his driver. "And let the others know that we might be making a stop."

There were four limousines in the caravan, each one identical with black exteriors and blacked out windows. Even the license plates were identical. From the outside, no one could tell one limousine from another—and that was just the way Rico had planned it. He was a man who believed in planning his work, then working his plan.

When they were thirty yards from the Lamborghini—and Rico could now see that it was this year's model—he saw that the front left tire was useless. It had been ripped to shreds because the driver had obviously driven several miles at considerable speeds with it being flat. The rim of the wheel was on the blacktop and looking much the worse for wear.

"When you get to her, stop. Let's see what's going on," Rico said.

The driver looked at him through the rearview mirror. He obviously didn't like the idea of stopping. Anything that deviated from the planned security protocol bother him greatly. And because it did, Rico trusted him completely, and paid him accordingly. Rico smile reassuringly.

Rico was in the lead car. He twisted to look out the tinted back window. The following three cars—one containing his younger brother, though he didn't know which one—were also pulling over to the shoulder of the road.

Rico's limousine came to a stop on the road's shoulder, well to the right of the Lamborghini, which was still in the middle of the right-hand lane.

Obviously, the driver of the Lamborghini expected everyone else to drive around her, not for her to be inconvenienced by pulling onto the shoulder.

Under normal circumstances, this kind of behavior would have bothered Rico enormously, especially if such selfishness had been exhibited by someone from the servant class. But she wasn't anyone's serf. Judging from the car to her clothes to her looks, everything about her screamed of aristocracy. Even from a distance she practically reeked of wealth.

The smell of it made Rico's libido take *intense* interest in the women with car trouble.

Rico felt his cock take notice of her financial and social status — and of her exquisite good looks. His cock had an infallible instinct for such matters, and always acted accordingly.

"Let me get out first and check things out," his bodyguard said.

"Of course," Rico replied. He knew his bodyguard was taking the right course of action, though Rico was anxious to get to know the woman and didn't want any delay. She was standing near the driver's door of her costly coupe, and she had a look on her face that said she was seriously pissed about the situation she was now in and that her mood was more likely to get worse than better.

As his bodyguard left the limousine, he grabbed the aluminum briefcase that had been on the seat beside him. Rico knew that none of his security men ever went anywhere without taking a briefcase with them. Inside each one was an Uzi submachine gun, with three extra thirty-shot magazines. Rico's men were armed to the teeth. It was a fact that gave Rico great comfort.

His bodyguards were all ex-military men, and they could

unleash the Hounds of Hell should anyone decide to be a threat to Rico or his brother. This caused Rico to sleep very easily at night.

Rico watched as his bodyguard talked for a moment or two with the tall blonde woman. Then the guard looked through the front window of the limousine, directly into Rico's eyes, and gave a nod. He then immediately took several steps backward.

I sure as hell hope I'm paying him what he deserves.

He decided the man was going to get a significant raise, starting immediately.

Rico got out of the limousine, made sure that his zipper was up and that his necktie was straight, and walked around the opened door to meet what he believed was one of the most beautiful women he'd ever seen in his life.

"My name's Rico Santiago, and I'm certainly hoping that I can help you." He spoke in English. She did *not* look Latin.

"You sure look like my knight in shining armor."

She spoke English with a distinct Russian accent. She smiled at him, and Rico's heart seized up just a little. He extended his hand so they could shake, but what he really want to do at that moment was to bend her over the hood of her low-slung sportster and fuck her from behind. He tamped down his desire, but didn't doubt that Tomas would find her beauty as intoxicating as he did. They had shared many women.

All eyes turned toward him as he spoke. "Whatever has gone wrong can be righted," he said. His smile was honest. He was a man long accustomed to making the world bend to his wishes, so he was quite certain he could fix whatever was not right in this woman's world.

"I cannot believe this has happened to me." The woman pointed at the destroyed tire as though its malfunction was an offense that she should take personally. "I almost never get to drive. All I wanted to do was drive for a while. I'm always in limousines or hotel rooms. I just wanted to drive fast and feel the air in my hair."

There aren't a hundred women in the world with eyes that blue.

"How far are we from Mexico City? My hotel is the Hotel Mexico International. Is there some way you would be kind enough to take me there?"

Rico shook his head. "My house is less than two kilometers away. We'll go there. I'll make some calls to have your car dealt with." He stepped closer. When he did he caught the classic, distinctive scent of Chanel No. 5. The perfume aroused him, triggering his masculine instincts. He liked women who knew how to be sensual without being trashy. Nothing said sophistication like a woman wearing Chanel No. 5. "Please, let me show you a safe harbor, and with a few phone calls, I'm sure we can make everything you want in life yours to enjoy."

She's Russian. That accent is unmistakable. And she's got some serious money behind her, or she wouldn't be driving a Lamborghini. What the hell is she doing here? Why haven't I known about her before now?

"By the way, I'm Svetlana."

Rico wanted to know a lot more about her than just that. He promised himself that he would have the answers to those questions before the sun went down. He hadn't become a billionaire by allowing his questions to be left unanswered.

CHAPTER SIX

Svetlana was introduced to Tomas by Rico, and right away, Rico could see that his brother found her attractive.

Good. He's always had a keen eye for beauty. I wonder if she's open to a ménage a trois.

The thought gave Rico a pause, and he inhaled deeply and slowly several times just to compose himself. It occurred to Rico that he hadn't been in Svetlana's company five minutes before she was bewitching his senses, tantalizing his libido, and basically making him pretty goddamned stupid. No woman had done that to him in such a short period of time in more years than Rico could remember.

"We'll take my car," Rico said, making sure his brother wouldn't jump to the front of the line. It had happened several times before, and it always pissed Rico off to the marrow of his bones when it did. "Let's get civilized, and we'll let those who do such things take care of all your problems." His smile was innocence itself. His English had almost no accent at all. He gave the utterly deceptive appearance of being the most innocent person alive.

He watched as the woman closed her eyes, tilted her face heavenward, and silently mouthed the words *thank you.* Then she looked him directly in the eyes and asked, "You're sure you don't mind?"

Rico thought, at that moment, that her Russian-accented English was just about the sexiest music he had ever heard. It was an aphrodisiac that acted immediately.

"It's my pleasure," Rico said.

Tomas stepped closer and said, "No, it's *our* pleasure."

Rico gritted his teeth. *I like sharing with him, but sometimes I want a bitch all to myself. At least to begin with.*

"Shall we go?" he said. He wanted to say much, much more, but he didn't.

"Let me get my purse," Svetlana replied.

Rico was watched when she bent forward at the waist to lean into the low-slung car through the open driver's side window. Her miniskirt pulled up even higher at the move, and Rico could see her legs almost to her panties.

Is she even wearing panties?

It was a tantalizing thought.

Fuck. I feel like I'm thirteen.

She came back, and by the time she did, lust was bombarding all of Rico's senses.

"You're sure I'm not keeping you from anything?" she asked. "I'll be ever so grateful."

He loved her Russian accent. He spoke English very well, and she said that though she spoke some Spanish, she didn't speak enough for them to communicate unless it was sexual.

"Sexual?" he asked. The smile on his lips hinted at unspoken pleasures.

"It is the universal language."

When she'd said that, as they were standing just outside his limousine, he knew with granite solid certainty that he had to keep her in his life for the near future. There couldn't be another woman like her in all the world.

He watched with unblinking interest as she eased herself into the back seat of his car. The miniskirt was short to begin with, but when she sat down, it pulled up even higher, showing off her legs almost to her bottom.

"With a man like you, I don't want to be a bother," Svetlana said, twisting so that she somewhat faced Rico in the back seat.

He thought her legs were nothing less than sheer

perfection. It was difficult for Rico to not stare at her breasts, which moved freely without a bra. The sheer white silk blouse she wore did hide their loveliness, but not their fullness, nor their distinctly aroused state. Her nipples were noticeably erect.

"Can I get you something to drink?" Rico asked. "I keep a rather well-stocked refrigerator in my cars. I spend so much time in them every day that I find it necessary to have food and beverages available at all times."

"Do you have vodka? Vermouth?" Her voice held anticipation. She was a woman who enjoyed her martini. Rico found her swift decision-making quite charming.

"I'm sorry to say that I have vodka, but I don't have any vermouth," Rico said after an awkward couple seconds of silence. "It's a mistake that will be corrected very soon."

"What are you having?"

"Tequila. Straight. Ice cold. I keep it in the freezer and pour it over ice."

Rico's heart skipped a beat when Svetlana put her hand on his thigh, touching him through his trousers. The touch was very light.

"I'll have what you're having. It'll be something that we can share." There was warmth in her tone.

Rico poured the drinks, and as he did, he wondered for the nth time whether the woman he had just met was wearing panties. The miniskirt she was wearing was provocatively daring, and with her sitting instead of standing, the bottom hem was at the tops of her thighs. Her beauty made it difficult to breathe.

Rico discovered himself smitten, like a teenager who was just learning the astonishing pleasures that were possible in the company of what he occasionally thought of as the *fairer sex*.

He looked up into the rearview mirror in the center of the

windshield, and found himself looking straight into the eyes of his bodyguard. Without exchanging a single word, he let the man know that he wanted to make the conclusion of the trip back to his mansion something that would take as long as possible. He had Svetlana to himself, *without* Tomas, and he wanted to keep it that way as long as possible.

"What brings you to Mexico City?" Rico asked, then opened a tequila. Though Svetlana was only half-finished with the small drink he'd made for her, he had no intention of letting her glass get anywhere near empty. "I don't think I've seen you before."

"I had to get away for a while, and since I don't know a single person in Mexico City, it seemed like the perfect place for me to go."

"You wanted to get away from it all?" Rico raised his eyebrows. "A little escape from life?"

"Precisely."

"In that case, I think you'll like my home. It is nothing if not private. Much more private than your hotel. It is humble, but it is comfortable." His home was the precise opposite of humble.

Svetlana looked at him over her glass of tequila on ice and said in a voice almost too soft to be heard, "I had thought my flat tire was the worst possible luck, but I'm beginning to think that the flat tire was the luckiest thing that's happened to me in a long, long time."

Rico could feel his cock begin to grow into an erection. It would be only a matter of seconds before she couldn't possibly remain unaware of his sexually aroused condition.

"How far away is your house?"

Rico heard the undercurrent in her tone, the sexual tension that she was trying to not let him know about. Lust, like a dangerous drug, surged through his veins and made him almost dizzy.

Rico began making plans to seduce Svetlana while she talked about her experience renting the car and the hassle it had been for her because she hadn't made a reservation for it and there was only one rental place *that rents cars worth driving.*

"It must have been difficult," Rico said quietly, with great sympathy, though all of it was false. "But you're here now, with my brother and me. Under our protection, you will have no worries." He leaned closer, over the center console, not stopping until the tips of their noses were almost touching. "When you are with me, you'll live the life of a czarina." He was choosing his noun carefully.

He felt the warmth of her breath as she sighed. He also felt his cock getting harder by the second. This Svetlana woman must have put some powerful aphrodisiacs into his veins. Of this he was certain.

He put his right palm lightly on the left side of Svetlana's face, and said in a voice in a husky whisper, "Your flat tire is the most fortune thing that's happened to me in years."

He kissed her then, half expecting her to protest. She did not. And when the tip of his tongue touched her lips, there was only momentary hesitation on her part before she opened her mouth and allowed him to French kiss her.

It was more than just a timid, tentative French kiss. She sucked on his tongue, drawing it more deeply into her mouth. Her tongue danced and caressed his with uninhibited zeal.

He put his right hand on her leg, on the warm, naked flesh of her left thigh. In response, Svetlana moaned softly into his mouth, and the erection Rico had previously sported immediately came fully to life. Rico felt a certain pride in the solidity.

She finally turned her face away to end the kiss, but not until after a full minute of deep, sensual tongue-dancing had taken place.

"Wait," she said in a breathy whisper. "This is happening

too fast."

Rico fought against the impulse to grab her by the hair, then force her to her knees on the floor of the limousine to give him a blow job. It most certainly wouldn't be the first time he'd done such a thing. It wouldn't be the second, third, or fourth time he'd made a reluctant woman give him a blow job. But Svetlana's clothes, and the Lamborghini, made Rico hold in check his more base, violent impulses. On most occasions, he never considered reining in his savage nature, but Svetlana's obvious wealth sent off warning bells deep within his brain. He didn't mind poor enemies, but rich enemies were something that had to be attended to.

If there was anything that Rico understood, and had from a very young age, it was that rich men could take their pleasures from young women as long as they were poor, but if the ladies were rich, then that might cause complications that weren't necessary, and should be avoided. It was a practical consideration, not a moral one.

"The driver," Svetlana said in a breathy whisper. "What about the driver? He can see us."

"He won't look, and he won't say a word." Rico paid his bodyguards enough money to make sure he was always safe, to look the other way when he wanted them to, and to keep their mouths shut regarding how and with whom their employers amused themselves.

He tried to pull Svetlana in closer, but the center console was in the way. When she resisted, her breasts trembled inside her silk blouse. He liked it when women struggled against his advances, though he loathed them when they continued to refuse his sexual demands.

So far, Svetlana had resisted enough to heighten his arousal, but not so much that she incited his rage. The difference between the two emotional states was as thin as a razor.

He watched as Svetlana looked first at the driver through

the glass barrier separating the passenger compartment from the driver's area, then out through the windshield. They had just crested a hill, and now his chalet was visible in the distance, all brick and granite and glass, two stories of architectural beauty designed at the turn of the previous century, exuding wealth and power and privilege, and as impressive today as it had been more than a hundred years earlier. Rico had learned as a child that it was always important to be impressive.

"Holy Mother of God . . . is that where you live?" Svetlana asked, speaking through her fingers because her hand was to her mouth.

It was the universal sign of being awestruck, and Rico was pleased.

"That's not a house, that's a castle."

Rico kept the smile to himself. Women often had that kind of response when they saw his house for the first time. Usually, though, the women were younger than Svetlana, and certainly not the sort who drove rented Lamborghinis. He looked at her profile and reminded himself that she wasn't the type of woman who could be abused, then paid off to keep her silence about what'd he'd done.

I'm going to fuck you. The thought was so clear in Rico's mind, it was as though he had spoken the words aloud. He looked down at her breasts, noticed how her nipples made prominent dents in the silk blouse, and told himself that, at least for now, he had to cool his ardor and show patience. The magnificence of his home might well be more seductive to someone like Svetlana than his own charismatic charm.

"It's beautiful, isn't it?"

Svetlana nodded, looking at the mansion in the distance. "How many people live there?"

"My brother and I, some servants, and some men who provide security."

His home had originally been built to be the clubhouse and hotel for an eighteen-hole golf course. It could easily house dozens of people. After buying the property, the brothers had a twenty-foot-high cyclone fence put up to surround the course, and had the fence electrified. There were flood lights with motion sensors strategically located. There was only one gate leading into and out of the property, and that was manned at all times by experienced former soldiers who were very familiar with the AK-47s that were kept out of sight but within easy reach at the guards' stations. Video cameras monitored all activity.

"My God . . . that is beautiful," Svetlana said, looking around at the almost endless expanse of rolling grassland that used to be a golf course. "I'm always in big, crowded cities. I never have any privacy. There's never any room. You . . . you have so much *space*."

Rico kept his smile to himself. He was quite confident that his home would provide all the foreplay he needed to get the luscious Russian named Svetlana into bed.

First I'll fuck her alone, and then I'll fuck her with Tomas.

Fucking her was a foregone conclusion. The only thing that Rico was unsure of was whether she'd scream with pleasure or pain when he and his brother did a forceful, vigorous double-penetration of her.

CHAPTER SEVEN

When they're here in this compound, they're invincible. They can't be touched. Not when they're at home. Electrified fence. Armed guards. Everything they need.

The thought came to Svetlana as the limousine slowed, approaching the gate that allowed passage into Rico's residence. At the guard's station there were two men. One was outside the small shack, waiting to greet the limousines. The other remained inside the shack.

There's only about a one hundred percent chance that he's got an assault rifle at the ready.

The limousines came to a stop, and the guard stepped up to the driver's side window. He smiled and nodded to the driver, then looked very briefly at Rico. When he looked at Svetlana, she was a little surprised that she didn't see sexual interest in his eyes. Instead, she saw suspicion. Her presence hadn't been anticipated, apparently, and he was obviously a man who didn't like surprises.

"Good afternoon, Señor Santiago." The guard hardly glanced at Rico. Svetlana saw that he was looking at her purse, and the expression on his face suggested that he didn't like what he saw. He looked European, which surprised Svetlana. "Señorita, may I please inspect your purse."

Svetlana shot Rico a glance carrying all the sense of victimhood she knew ultra-rich possessed whenever they had to behave by the same rules that the rest of the world must.

"Please, my dear," Rico said, his smile benevolent. "It is just a formality that all guests must endure. Trust me, I'll make up for this offence as soon as we get settled in my home."

Svetlana slipped the strap off her shoulder and handed the small purse to the guard. He thumbed open the catch, and when he looked inside, she watched his eyes widen and his expression turn stony-hard.

"I'll have to keep this for now," he said in a voice without emotion. "Provided Señor Santiago allows it, you can have this back later."

He stepped away from the limousine, and made a motion to the man inside the small building. A moment later the gate was raised, and then the armored cars were driving the last hundred yards to the chalet.

"What was in your purse?" Rico asked.

"A gift from Daddy," Svetlana replied, then smiled coyly and looked out the side window away from Rico.

"What kind of gift?"

"A gold-plated one," Svetlana said.

"Those are always nice gifts."

She smiled at him and briefly raised her slender eyebrows naughtily. "Mine is a gold-plated twenty-five caliber Browning automatic. It was for my birthday."

She saw the surprise in his eyes, and she knew that she had just deepened the mystery of herself that she had wanted to create.

"You feel the need to keep a pistol with you?"

"Daddy feels I should have one." She looked down and grinned, then up into his eyes. "He says it is better to have a gun and not need it, then to need one and not have it."

"Your father is a very wise man." Rico put his hand on Svetlana's thigh, his fingers splayed, the tip of his little finger less than an inch from the crotch of her thong panties. "I'd like to meet him some day."

Without reacting either favorably or unfavorably to the

hand on her naked thigh, Svetlana replied, "Perhaps. Perhaps." *That'll make him curious as hell.*

And that was what Svetlana had hoped for when the mission began.

It would take a battalion of men to effectively attack this place. The only successful attack would have to be a smart bomb from a stealth plane.

It was not a comforting thought for Svetlana to have as she stood outside the limousine at the front entrance to the chalet. She was pretending to be looking at the grounds and the endless green lawn, but what she was really paying attention to were the gun turrets that were shrouded in netting to hide them from aerial videography. She suspected there were machine guns in those turrets. Probably military-grade weapons, with enough ammunition to create a hell on earth for whoever tried to get past the electrified gate without an invitation.

Every soldier in the world was afraid of a .50-caliber Browning machine gun mounted on a tripod.

"It's beautiful," Svetlana said quietly to Rico. She took his hand in hers and gave it an affectionate squeeze. "Thank you for bringing me here. I feel like I've been rescued."

"A flat tire can happen to anyone." His tone was neutral, but he kept hold of Svetlana's hand. He clearly had no intentions of letting go of it any time soon.

"Do you know what a Lamborghini costs to rent for a week? At that price, I'd better not get a damned flat tire." She was pleased with the upper-class, aggrieved tone of her voice. She was familiar with the role she was playing. "And you're sure you can help me with the car? You know someone?"

"Give me a few minutes. I have some calls to make, and then everything will be made well again." He took a half-step closer.

Svetlana thought that he was going to kiss her. He didn't, but she knew he had wanted to, and that she would have let him. She knew what the mission required.

He took her hand as she got out of the car. They headed for the front door, and he continued to hold her hand. She did not resist.

"Perhaps you'd like a drink before I leave. Maybe that vodka martini that I was unable to provide in the car?"

"No, that's not necessary."

"It might not be necessary, but all of us want more than just bare sustenance." He walked to a wheeled cart containing an assortment of liquor bottles. He poured vodka and vermouth into a stainless-steel shaker, added ice, capped it with another shaker, then shook vigorously. "Señorita Svetlana, let me know what you think about this." He handed Svetlana the martini.

When she took a sip of it, she closed her eyes and sighed softly. Rico was most assuredly a murderous bastard who deserved a slow, painful death, but he made a magnificent martini. *Even bastards can have talent that's useful.*

"Make your calls," Svetlana said, "and let me sit by the windows and enjoy my martini. But don't take too much time. I'm learning to enjoy your company." She took a sip of her drink. "And I'm finding you curiously amusing."

"That's curious?"

She looked at him and said frankly, "Most men bore me. You don't. I find that both curious and amusing."

There was nothing less that pure lust shining in his eyes.

It was all that she could have hoped for.

He didn't make the calls himself, of course. He gave the assignment to have the Lamborghini taken care of to one of his men, with the specific instructions that the repair to the tire was not to be done immediately. The work should be completed the following day, and not before noon, at the earliest.

Actually, around three o'clock in the afternoon would be about right, he said. And if it got closer to five, that wouldn't make him angry at all. Rico was in no hurry for Svetlana to have the freedom to go where she wished.

"So what do you think?" Rico asked his younger brother. "She did have a gun."

"Many interesting women have guns. Besides, it wasn't really much of a gun," Tomas replied, then grinned. "Have we gotten a report regarding her passport?"

A well-used, much-stamped passport had been in her purse, along with an international driver's license. There had been some paper money, but not enough to draw attention. It was the passport that was important. With it, Rico didn't need Svetlana to tell him who she was. He could find out for himself. There was a significant fortune in diamonds on her, with diamond studs in her ears that were at least three carats each.

"I just got it, and you're not going to believe what you're about to hear." There was a brightness in Tomas's eyes that was seldom there.

Rico felt himself tighten up inside. "Is it bad?" He was hoping with all his heart and soul that it wasn't. He couldn't remember wanting anything or anyone as much as Svetlana Simonov. She was in a league by herself.

"Bad? Brother, it's better than good. It's fucking fantastic."

Rico leaned forward in his chair, put his elbows on his office desk, and tried to pretend that he wasn't as anticipatory as he really was.

"Her name's Svetlana Simonov, she's twenty-eight, and for the past ten years she's been flying around the world, living in the finest five-star hotels that cater to her every whim, drinking the most expensive champagne on the planet . . . but she has no apparent source of income. And nobody had heard a word about her until she turned eighteen. Then *bam*. She's a major player in the jet set crowd. And everyone who counts has wanted her to join their party."

Rico's brows furrowed. "You're saying she's not really who she says she is?"

"In all likelihood, the first eighteen years of her life she lived under an alias, probably in a boarding school somewhere in Europe. Once she turned eighteen and got out of boarding school, it seems she reclaimed her own identity. She took the name she was apparently born under."

Rico recognized the teasing smiled on his little brother's face. "Spill it all. Don't keep me in suspense."

"She's Svetlana Simonov. Her mother was something or other Simonov. But she's probably the illegitimate daughter of one of the founding fathers of the Russian Mafia. You know, the one in hiding. We can't prove it, but that's what the smart money is saying."

"I thought he was dead. Nobody has seen him in years."

"He disappeared, but that doesn't mean he's dead." Tomas said it with a noticeable amount of disrespect.

"If he's alive, and we can use Svetlana as a conduit to the Russian Mafia, have you any idea what a profitable person Svetlana could be to our lives?"

"Of course I do," Tomas replied, grinning boyishly. "And she's in our lives all because of a flat tire on a rented Lamborghini."

Rico looked at his younger brother, who was smiling charmingly, and felt his own protective walls come up in an instant. If there was anything he knew about Tomas, it was that he couldn't trust him when it came to women. It was when Tomas was most charming that he was most dangerous.

He's going to want to fuck her first, but I'm not going to let him. I get her first, and then we can share her.

Rico loved his younger brother, but he hated him more than a little sometimes.

"So what did they say?" Svetlana asked, sitting back in a large wing-backed chair in front of a bank of floor-to-ceiling windows that looked out over what had used to be the first hole fairway of the golf course, but was now just a beautiful expanse of imported Kentucky blue-green grass.

"I'm afraid it's not going to be so easy as just changing a tire," Rico answered. He sat in a chair next to hers. "It seems that those folks at Lamborghini use very special, very rare tires, and none of the nearby shops have one in stock to replace your flat. They've got to special order it, so it'll take until tomorrow morning before you get your car back."

Svetlana let out a string of obscenities. "I'll need a ride back to my hotel."

"You could stay here for the night."

"Yes, I could, but we both know that if I did, we'd end up having sex." She sighed in an elaborate, resigned sort of way. "And as delightful as that would be, I'm not going to let it happen tonight. I've just met you, and I'm on the rebound from a relationship that ended disastrously."

"And that's why you're in Mexico City, where nobody knows you."

"It keeps the questions I get down to a minimum." She gave him something resembling a smile. "Nobody asks probing questions of a stranger."

"Can I at least feed you before I have my car take you to your hotel?"

Svetlana gave her head a little shake, then let Rico see a soft, flirtatious grin. "You have a beautiful limousine," she said.

"Four of them. All identical. With the windows thoroughly blacked out. That way nobody can tell whether I'm in the car, whether my brother's in the car, of if both of us are inside. Sometimes, neither one of us even leave the chalet, but the authorities—who are always sniffing around, trying to find something to charge us with—never know a damned thing. But all four limousines leave every day."

Svetlana said, "You're smarter than they are."

"I get the feeling you wanted to tell me something other than that I have a nice fleet of limousines."

"Promise you won't tease me?"

"Of course not. Never."

"Gorgeous cars and gorgeous men make me weak and wet." She closed her eyes, then drank the last of her vodka martini. "When I saw the Lamborghini at the rental place, my attraction to it was literally sexual. When I was driving it, my panties got soaked. Going through the gears was as good as masturbation. That's why it was so infuriating to get the flat tire. It was like finding out at the last minute that the man you want to ravage you senseless is impotent. He's all show and no go." She opened her eyes wide. "Tell me you're a stud. Please, tell me."

Rico looked at her for several seconds before responding. "When it comes to sex, I've always believed that there are talkers and there are doers. If you talk and brag about it, you probably don't perform. If you don't feel the need to sing your own praises, then in all likelihood, you leave women with a smile on their face when they fall asleep afterward."

"Oh . . . my," Svetlana whispered, "I've never heard it put quite that way, but that's the best explanation I've ever heard."

She watched as Rico smiled, and she could sense his self-confidence, which had always been high, growing even more. What she also knew was that the more confident he was, the less likely he was to sense the trap that she needed to lure him into if her mission was to succeed.

"Your glass is empty," Rico said. "Can I make you at least one more?"

Svetlana looked at her empty martini glass for several seconds without saying a word. She pressed her lips together for a moment as though deliberating the pros and cons of her next decision.

"Just one more, but then you've got to take me home." As Rico took the martini glass, she looked into his eyes and asked, "But you *will* accompany me back to the hotel, won't you? You won't just give your driver orders to take me back to my room?"

"My limousine is roomy enough for the two of us," Rico said, his tone and words full of double entendre. "And it's very comfortable and quiet. We'll be able to talk. Besides, I would never send you home alone.

Like hell we'll be able to talk. You want to have one hell of a lot more from me than just a lively conversation.

That lousy, low-life motherfucker.

Tomas knew that Rico was anything but low life, but at the moment, that didn't really matter.

One of the bodyguards had just explained to Tomas that his older brother had recently left with Svetlana in a car. And since neither of them ever went anywhere without all four of the black SUVs going at the same time — for security purposes — then Rico had effectively escaped the chalet with Svetlana at his side.

Leaving Tomas behind. Alone. As intended.

I wanted her first.

He tried to remind himself that had been planning on secreting Svetlana away so that *he* could have sex with her first, before he shared her with his older brother. It didn't bother him to realize that he had been plotting to be just as treacherous as his brother. It did bother him that Rico had out-foxed him on this one.

If ever there was anyone that Tomas was uber-competitive

with, it was Rico. And the fact that more often than not, To-mas came out on the losing end of the competition infuriated him down to where his soul met his psyche, and the nerves that joined the two were always raw.

"Did anyone say when he'd be back?" Tomas asked, wondering if there was a glimmer of hope. But he knew there wasn't.

The servant—a man whose duties required him to often carry a pistol in a holster under his left arm and be ready at all times to kill anyone who posed a threat to either of the Señor Santiagos—shook his head slowly. There wasn't a single emotion visible in his eyes.

He was worth everything he was paid.

"And this is identical to the one the President of the United States has?" Svetlana ran her hand over the soft, leather seat of the limousine. When she looked up at Rico, she could see that he was ruddy-faced with passion, and that his ego was racing out of control because she was pretending to be impressed by something he owned. In truth, she couldn't give a rat's ass.

You own an armada of custom-made armored vehicles . . . but I own you. You just don't know it yet.

"You're sure I can't get you another drink?" Rico asked. He was just a little too solicitous to sound genuine, and Svetlana picked up on it. Those weren't the signs in men she always noticed immediately.

She had already observed that the four limousines were traveling noticeably slower than the surrounding traffic. Rico had been stretching his time with her. That was what she had wanted, though she hadn't known it when the mission had begun.

But she knew it now.

Svetlana handed Rico her glass, and he smiled cryptically.

"No. No more for me," Svetlana said quickly. She had slurred her words slightly, exaggerating the effect the liquor had on her. She knew how to play this game. "I have something much more entertaining than cocktails in mind." She let the tip of her tongue moisten her lips, and watched as Rico's eyes widened when she did. "How much longer until we get to my hotel?"

"As long as you want it to take."

Rico's words came out with machine-gun speed. His wishes were unmistakable. For only a moment Svetlana closed her eyes and summoned her willpower to give her strength.

Svetlana shook her head slowly. "It can't be more than fifteen minutes. Promise?"

She could see the gears turning in Rico's head. He didn't want to make a promise he wouldn't keep, but he had an opportunity presented to him that couldn't be resisted. After several seconds, and clearly hesitant to agree to Svetlana's wishes, he finally nodded.

"In that case, let me indulge a fantasy. I've made out in limousine, but never close to a Presidential limousine. That's something I want to do . . . and I want to do it with you." She looked him in the eyes. "Often."

Rico still had his cocktail glass when Svetlana moved both swiftly and acrobatically, blithely tossing her glass to the carpeted floor. One second she was sitting in the back seat of the limousine, facing forward and sipping her martini with a center console separating her from Rico. In the next she was facing backward, having moved around the center console. Her thighs were spread wide apart, and her knees were on the luxurious leather back seat as she straddled the billionaire's hips.

Without hesitation. Svetlana cupped Rico's face in her hands. She angled his face upward, then planted a firm, deep, soulful kiss on his lips.

In the back of her mind, she was conscious of hearing two glasses falling to the carpeted floor of the limousine, and neither one made the sound of breaking. The carpeting was thick. An instant after that she heard Rico moan deep in his throat when she put her tongue in his mouth. By spreading her knees so wide apart to straddle his waist, she had caused her miniskirt to ride up very high, past her hips.

His hands were cupping her buns almost immediately. She had surprised him by her bold move, but he was quick on the uptake. She felt the tips of his fingers slide beneath the leg seams of her panties so that he could caress her intimately without obstructions. *He's mine now.*

Svetlana ended the kiss, then turned her face aside, availing her neck to his mouth. He did as she had hoped he would, biting and kissing her throat, but when he used his teeth too harshly on her, ninety percent of the eroticism of the moment evaporated in an instant. He didn't know how to be dominant without being abusive . . . and Svetlana wanted to spit in his face because of it.

There were very few men skillful enough in that kind of seduction in the world, and Svetlana was disappointed but not surprised that Rico wasn't one of them. Men who knew how to do that were as rare as thick veins of pure gold in a towering mountain.

She whispered, "Don't penetrate. There's only so far I'm willing to go."

With his mouth pressed against Svetlana's throat, Rico groaned. "You're so hot, so . . ." His words died away, and when he started speaking again, he spoke in garbled Spanish. The fact that she couldn't understand precisely what he was saying affected her not at all. She didn't need to understand his words, only to feel his touch, to understand what she needed to know.

She felt the fingers of his right hand slide closer to her

vagina, and a warning bell sounded in her brain. When he continued beneath her panties, searching, trying to touch her more intimately, she put her lips close to his ear and whispered, "I'm not willing to go that far tonight. Tomorrow, my darling. Tomorrow."

She felt his entire body tense up.

This is a man who doesn't let women say no to him.

The thought made Svetlana squeeze her eyes tightly shut, and clench her teeth in fury — because she knew that there was too much truth to her last thought.

This was a monster she'd enjoy clipping out at the knees.

"Tomorrow," she whispered. "Send your car for me. Be in the car. You know what fancy cars do to me."

Angrily, Rico replied, "But we're in the car now."

"It's too soon for me. Tomorrow."

"I'll be driving around Mexico City for six hours. Why not now?"

Svetlana stroked his hair and squirmed in his lap. She could feel his erection pressing against her.

"Why be happy with a few minutes, when you can have me in this lovely limousine for six hours? Just think how many times you can have your fun with me in six hours." She nibbled on his earlobe. "And I'm not squeamish. You can take whatever you want."

She felt him relax then, and Svetlana knew that she had won.

She also knew that she was going to pay a price for her victory the next morning.

Chapter Eight

He saw the lights of his chalet, and he knew that there was going to be hell to pay. Sneaking off with Svetlana had been a pretty tricky move, Rico acknowledged, but it wasn't like Tomas had never pulled a fast one himself.

But, all in all, Rico was feeling pretty good about the day. He had met Svetlana, and she had turned out to be erotic as hell, though a little odd, and in some ways quite diabolically dangerous. The whole concept of getting turned on when she was in a limousine wasn't the first time that Rico had such an encounter, but usually the women with fetishes had more pressing problems to deal with.

I wonder if she's into bondage? What about spanking? I'd love to drag her across the floor by her hair.

Fairly explicit thoughts of putting Svetlana over his knee, raising her miniskirt, taking down her panties, and giving her a sincerely-delivered bare-bottom spanking slithered across the surface of his mind like the serpent in the Garden of Eden.

She left me with blue balls. No bitch has left me with blue balls in years.

But Svetlana had. She had writhed on his lap and ground her pussy against his erection through his trousers and kissed him like she couldn't get enough of his tongue . . . but still she left him without a climax, which would have made a really nice end to the evening.

Rico thought about his itinerary for the next day. He had a full day scheduled. There were the meetings at two banks, and one at the construction company which was loosely scheduled for ten. Or was it eleven? And then, most importantly, there was his stop to the laboratory.

He smiled. He and Tomas thought of it as Dr. Frankenstein's laboratory, where scientists were creating a monster. A monster made out of microscopic virus cells that, from inside the human body, could multiply with astonishing speed, and the lethality would be stupendous. The infection rate was supposed to be at least triple of what the previous pandemic virus rates were.

And all Rico and his brother had needed to do was get the right three infectious disease scientists together, build them a laboratory in a large, empty building made out of seventy-year-old wood in the warehouse district of Mexico City, and promise them three million American dollars each if they could invent a virus that could wipe out half the population of the United States.

The scientists were only too happy to take on the assignment, provided each of them got two hundred thousand dollars American currency up front and the laboratory got built exactly to their specifications.

Considering the cash flow of the Santiago siblings were currently enjoying, the up-front money was chump change.

Inspection is tomorrow. Rico shook his head. Svetlana's beauty had addled his brain. He smiled to himself. *Tomorrow I'll fuck her. And after that she'll introduce us to her father, and the brothers Santiago will be in a whole new league.*

Svetlana looked at herself in the mirror, and was at least reasonably pleased with what she saw. She had showered, then blow dried her hair. After that she put on her eyelashes, and finally makeup.

Now she was naked, made up properly, and plotting her next move.

She looked at her wristwatch. It was gold-plated, with

diamonds to signify the individual hours. She'd had it for several years. The wristwatch was telling her that she had one hour before Rico would show up at her door to take her with him on his business rounds.

I promised him a good time. I said his limousine put me in the mood to have sex.

Svetlana knew she had been exaggerating about the limousine and her libido — but only a little. There was enough of an exhibitionist in her to find it erotic to be having sex while driving through the streets of a populous city. And if there happened to be a chauffeur in the car, well, that didn't exactly put a damper on her ardor — provided he knew that he could watch what she was doing in the back seat, but he wasn't allowed to invite himself in on the activities.

And let's face it, Rico isn't an ugly man. In fact, he's pretty handsome. He's a murderous bastard who needs to die as quickly as possible if the world is spinning the way it is supposed to . . . but he really isn't bad looking at all.

Svetlana accepted, with a certain amount of resignation, that she had responsibilities that she'd agreed to take on, and she must now fulfill those responsibilities. Her beauty was to her what a rifle was to a sniper.

So, how to dress to meet Rico and put him completely under my spell?

The initial thing Svetlana realized was that being fully dressed and ready for a busy day wasn't the first choice. It wasn't in the top ten choices. Equally true was that being buck-assed naked and looking like she was ready to get laid in the next thirty seconds wouldn't get her the response she wanted. No, this was going to take a rather more sophisticated, subtle approach.

Panties. Gotta wear panties. Way too obvious if not wearing panties. Svetlana smiled to herself. *Though I do sort of like it when I go commando. Walking around in a miniskirt or mini dress without panties when no one knows it but me makes me wet.*

She went to the chest of drawers where all of the clothes in the world that she owned were. She had two very large, hard-shelled, wheeled suitcases, and in them were her worldly possessions. Everything had been provided by Omega Force.

When Svetlana arrived at a hotel with her suitcases, it was the equivalent of a college student coming back to her parents' home and unpacking everything she owned.

She hadn't really had a home in a decade. Not since she'd joined Omega Force, and everything that she thought she knew about her life got turned upside down.

Panties. Concentrate. Panties.

All of her panties had a matching brassiere. And most of those pairs had a matching garter belt. Even if the rest of the world wasn't aware of it, Svetlana liked knowing that she was wearing very pretty, feminine, sexy lingerie. And they all matched. Always.

She checked out a lacy black thong, but decided that it wouldn't do because thongs were never as comfortable as bikini panties. And the choices were only between thong or bikini, because she sure as hell wasn't going to wear granny panties, or those boy shorts that truly disgusted Svetlana to the very marrow of her feminine soul. She didn't give a damn what some Hollywood starlets decided to wear and then show the world.

So, what is it going to be? There's only one chance to make a first impression, so it has to be the right *first impression.*

She settled on a robin's egg blue blouse with a knee-length dark blue skirt suit, garter belt, and stockings. She'd project a solidly professional appearance.

People are going to look at me and think I'm his over-paid, high-priced lawyer, and Rico will get a hard-on.

No matter which way Svetlana looked at this, it seemed like a win-win situation, because the over-priced attorney persona not only made her feel powerful, it also made her feel sexy . . . and with a man as loathsome as Rico, she needed external influences to help shovel the coal to stoke the fire of desire. Svetlana had long ago learned the value of setting the stage in order to act in the play as it was written.

As though carefully arranging a flower bouquet, Svetlana set out her bikini panties, brassiere, garter belt, and then her white thigh-high silk stockings. She put them all on the edge of the bed. She placed them there, then took several steps back to look at them from a distance.

Yes, that'll make a nice first impression. He'll know I'm trying to be pretty for him. Pretty, but not slutty.

She walked over to her closet, where her robes hung on thick, plastic hangers that would hold them securely but not make creases. She had several choices and they ranged from a rather bulky terry cloth robe that covered from the neck to the ankles, to sheer silk robes that came down only to the tops of her thighs.

Svetlana decided on a black robe that barely covered the essentials and wouldn't allow its wearer to bend over at the waist without showing ass cheeks — and even more than that. She felt sexy in it.

Black looks good against my pale skin. But, Jesus, that shows an awful lot of leg, and if I move bend over, he's going to learn that I wax. Maybe I should go without a bra. Sheesh. My boobs are going to be bouncing.

Considering what was at stake, this was not the time to make her moves to be half-measures.

She decided on the black shorty silk robe.

She put on her garment, then sat on the edge of her bed and began to hope like hell that Rico wouldn't be late, because the suspense was killing her. She'd always hated waiting. She knew that her impatience was a weakness, but her willpower was usually enough to counter it.

At precisely eight o'clock, the phone on her bedside table rang. It was the front desk, and there were men who wanted to see her. Were they allowed to come up?

Men? Damn. I wasn't counting on anyone other than Rico.

Svetlana thought that it was probably just Rico's bodyguards with him. He never went anywhere without them.

No need to worry. It's all cool.

Only, when they arrived, it wasn't all cool. It wasn't just Rico and his bodyguards who arrived at her door, it was Rico and Tomas, along with their four bodyguards.

And Svetlana was wearing a gossamer-thin silk robe that did absolutely nothing to hide the shape of her body—or the fact that she wasn't wearing anything beneath it. She wished she were anywhere else on the planet.

"Oh," she said, looking at the brothers. "Oh, damn."

"Can we enter?" Rico asked. There was an amused twinkle in his eyes, which Svetlana wasn't really all that pleased about. Having both brothers and all their bodyguards show up at her hotel door was not the way she had planned for this morning to begin—and now she had no idea how the day would progress.

In a very soft voice, Svetlana asked, "All of you?"

Now both Rico and Tomas smiled, and Svetlana began to feel a little better. Not much better, but a little. She figured any emotional movement in the right direction was a good thing.

"No," Rico said. "Just Tomas and me. Our men can stay in the hallway."

Svetlana looked at the soldiers. The four of them were carrying stainless steel briefcases, and had that look of men who hadn't had a rollicking good belly laugh since they were in kindergarten.

Men like that frightened Svetlana. She already had too many of them in her life, and she wasn't interested in having any more.

It just seemed like she didn't have any real choice in the matter, and that was the worst part of it.

"You're sure. That seems rude," she said, pretending to be ignorant of the fact that for centuries people in Svetlana

Simonov's social position were rude to the servant class all the time, and never felt a twinge of regret.

"Trust me, they understand," Rico said.

Tomas asked, in as polite a voice as Svetlana had ever heard, "Can we come in?"

She looked at Tomas and felt a shiver slither up her spine. He was shorter than his older brother, but more handsome. His hair was longer, curling well over his collar, and though his eyes were dark like Rico's, there was a brightness about them that was enticing. And when he smiled, there was a dimple in his cheek—and Svetlana had always had a soft spot in her libido for anyone with dimples. There was a distinctly Latin sexiness to him that Svetlana had not noticed earlier, but was distinctly aware of now.

"Oh, yes," Svetlana answered after a moment. She stepped aside and opened the door wide. "Of course."

She was immediately and embarrassingly aware of her body, of how voluptuous it was, and of how paper-thin silk robe did *nothing*—as in *fucking nothing*—to keep her breasts from trembling, jiggling, swaying, and generally making an attention-getting nuisance of themselves every time she took so much as a single step. She felt as though she was being scrutinized—because she was.

"I'm sorry, but I'm not quite dressed yet," she said, her back to the men, who were standing just inside her door. It didn't help that they were immaculately and properly dressed, handsome as hell, and precisely the kind of men that she was never supposed to have anything in her heart but contempt for.

"We've still got a little time," Rico said. "You've got at least fifteen minutes."

Svetlana's eyes opened wide. "Fifteen minutes? Do you know how little time that is?" It was a complaint.

She watched when, in the flicker of a moment, a fury

appeared and then disappeared in Tomas's eyes. And in that fraction of a second, she knew everything she needed to know about him. He was dangerous. He was a killer. He was a man who took what he wanted in life and didn't give a damn if someone else didn't like it. He frightened her.

"Will you please turn your back?" She gave them a smile that she hoped was sweet, and just a little apologetic. "I'm afraid me and schedules have never been really good friends. I'm late more often than I'm not." She sighed. "I'm sorry, and I apologize."

"I can cure that," Rico said, and after he had, Svetlana knew that she hated him, and that she always had to keep that hatred in the forefront of her consciousness. He was a man who made others bend to his will. She would be foolish to have any other emotion regarding him other than contempt.

She unknotted the slender sash of her robe, and then, standing barely fifteen feet from the men, turned her back on them and let the silk drift off her shoulders and slither down her arms.

Be calm. You can do this.

She stepped into the bikini panties first. She was hellishly curious whether they were looking, but she didn't turn to try to catch them spying.

Next she put on a demi bra that perfectly matched her panties and had the lovely, ornate trimming along the upper edges of the cups that barely controlled the fullness of her bosom. The closure was between the cups. It would make it easier for the men to undo her bra, and now—with Tomas there—Svetlana wasn't at all certain she had made the right choice.

It's too damned late for second guesses.

"No peeking now," she said, because she suspected the men expected her to say something like that.

She put her garter belt on and snaked the straps under her panties. To roll the stockings up her legs she had to sit on the foot of the bed. This allowed her to cast a quick glance at the men. She was relieved that they weren't looking at her.

It was early morning, but already the day had gone straight to hell.

"Well, at least now I'm not naked," Svetlana said, struggling to find some levity.

The men turned around to face her. She didn't make eye contact.

She rolled up her stockings and could feel the heat and lust of the brothers as they looked at her. She did not look back. She was struggling to reclaim some of her own power, and she was determined to hold it securely in her own hands.

When she had finished attaching the last back garter clasp — which required her to be a contortionist — to her stocking, she stood and turned her back on the brothers. She asked in an innocent tone, "Are the seams straight?"

She knew perfectly well how incendiary her question was. A moment later, she heard the men — who were both experienced in the ways of debauchery — inhale deeply and then hold their breath for a moment. She felt that she might have turned the tide. She had turned the momentum so that things were at last going somewhat her way.

Seconds passed before she heard Rico, in a tone that was clearly strained, say, "Yes, the seams are straight."

They're not the icebergs that they pretend to be. They're just as susceptible as any other man. They just pretend they aren't.

With that in mind, and knowing that they were visually devouring her every move, Svetlana turned so that she faced them, then bent over slowly at the waist to pick her blouse up off the mattress. Aware that she was being watched closely, she moved slowly. She could feel their sexual hunger.

Without arrogance or temerity, Svetlana had known from her teen years that she had breasts that were something more than what other girls possessed. They weren't just larger. Larger didn't mean prettier — larger just referred to size.

Svetlana's breasts were simply beautiful, and she knew it. She was aware of this from the very beginning. They were full, round, with areolas the color of coffee heavily laced with cream. The edges of the areolas were hardly discernible from the flesh of her breasts, and Svetlana always thought this a detriment, something that wasn't quite as it should be, but when she said this to her friends, they argued vociferously to convince her otherwise. And both boys and girls, men and woman, could place a hand on a Bible and swear under oath that Svetlana's breasts were the most beautiful of all time. A lie detector machine would prove their honesty. They were all willing to take that test.

And then there were those people who claimed her ocean blue eyes could not be matched in beauty by anyone, anywhere, at any time.

That was the kind of certainty Svetlana inspired, but she was always a bit embarrassed by it.

With her back still to the men, Svetlana picked up her blouse, slipped her arms through the sleeves, and began buttoning it. As her fingers manipulated the little plastic buttons, she could *literally* feel the heat of the twin gazes of the Santiago brothers on the cheeks of her ass.

When she finished with her blouse, she picked up the knee-length rather modest skirt and stepped into it.

"When I was a little girl," Svetlana said, her voice whisper-soft but evocative, "I dreamed of having a personal maid who would dress me correctly—you know, in proper Russian style—but that never happened." She chuckled softly, self-deprecatingly. "If that isn't the ultimate first-world problem, then I don't know what is." She laughed a little, this time self-deprecatingly. "You're living a charmed life when all of your problems are first-world."

She put on her skirt, pulled it up and tucked in her blouse, zipped up the skirt, then picked up her jacket and pulled it on. She could feel the way every move she made was being watched.

The earlier fears that had gripped her soul were gone. She was dressed now, and when she looked at Rico and Tomas, she knew that they lusted after her — and that awareness gave her a sense of power. Her time in Omega Force had taught her that being lusted after was a professional asset.

"Well now, gentlemen, how shall we proceed with this day?"

She was trying to sound casual, nonchalant, and she had succeeded brilliantly. When she looked at the Santiago brothers, she could see that they were shocked with her bold behavior, and her confidence went up accordingly. Shocked men weren't thoughtful men. She was on the sharply upward angle of a learning curve.

She watched as Rico clearly his throat and Tomas looked at his older brother, seeking advice on just exactly what the next move should be.

"Do I have both of you to myself?"

"Not for the beginning of the day," Rico said. "Tomas has separate stops that he has to make. But we'll all be getting together later on."

She smiled. "Well, the three of us being together part of the day is better than none of the day."

CHAPTER NINE

The drive in the limousine began with Rico and Svetlana sitting in the forward-facing seats with the center console between them. They chatted as the limousine made its way slowly through the congested traffic. Then Rico got out of his seat and crossed over to the rearward-facing bench seat. He reached a hand toward Svetlana.

She took it and let him pull her onto the bench seat. Seconds later they were doing what kids called heavy petting, others called making out, and others call foreplay. Svetlana had another term for it, though she tended to not speak it aloud. That was just as well.

"This is ridiculous," Svetlana said as she pushed herself away from Rico. "I mean, you know that, don't you?"

They were headed for Rico's first appointment, though Svetlana didn't know where that was. She hadn't even actually asked, because she knew he wouldn't answer. But her senses were on high alert for any clue he might let slip.

Svetlana put her hand over the significant lump in Rico's trousers, gave it a firm squeeze, and asked, "Is this thing always hard, or is it just me?"

She looked into Rico's eyes, waited a moment, then gave him a smile. Then she gave him a more intimate squeeze.

Rico said, "It's you."

Her smile broadened. "Good answer. I know you're lying through your teeth, but that's the right answer." She squeezed him even more firmly, and even ran her palm up and down over his arousal. "Now how much time do we have to reach your first appointment?"

Rico looked at his wristwatch, blinking his eyes several times, then finally said, "Ten minutes."

"Then I'm going to suck your cock for the next eight minutes." Her eyes narrowed. "And if you come this early in the day, I might kill you . . . and there isn't a jury of women in Mexico who would convict me." She kissed his mouth briefly. "We're going for a marathon here, not a sprint to the finish."

With deft fingers she pulled down the zipper to Rico's fly, then reached inside. She looked up and saw that Rico's eyes were the size of saucers. Then she paid closer attention to what her hands were doing. Almost the instant her fingers wrapped around the shaft of his cock, his whole body started to shiver slightly. Svetlana wasted no time. She had enough history in such matters to know that a man was much easier to get out through the fly of his trousers when he was pliant, than when his cock had all the flexibility of a flagpole. She had succeeded in what she had planned to do.

"Fuck," Rico said quietly, when Svetlana had pulled his cock out through his fly.

"Later. Right now I'm just priming the pump and getting your heart started." She smiled at him, then leaned upward enough to kiss him on the point of his chin. "Fucking comes later. We're just playing around." She laughed throatily. "But trust me, you're going to enjoy yourself." She kissed the corner of his mouth. "Just remember we're not near the finish line."

"Jesus," Rico said.

"Enjoy yourself, but don't blaspheme. I don't like that." A moment later she wrapped her lips around the shaft of his cock, taking the rapidly growing crown completely into her mouth. She moaned. The sound was only partially theatrical.

Svetlana began bobbing slowly up and down, and as she did, she drew a very firm suction on a cock that as awakening now that it was being shown attention, but was not yet near a full erection.

It didn't stay at half-mast for long. Rico might have been surprised by Svetlana's bold behavior, but once her mouth engulfed his cock, his virility had leaped to DefCon 6, his blood was pumping like a fire hose straight into that part of his body that most needed a healthy supply of fresh blood.

And all this happened in just a couple seconds.

"That's so good," Rico said as his now-rigid cock slid between Svetlana's lips until the head of his arousal was pressing against the opening of her throat. He said something else in a Spanish dialect that Svetlana did not understand, but even though she didn't know what the words meant, she knew what the sentiment was. And that was all that was important.

He put a hand atop her head, but didn't try to influence her flux and flow movements. Instead, he just caressed her hair between his fingers and thumb, and the feel of his gentle touch gave her pleasure.

Svetlana moaned softly and worked her tongue against the slit at the tip of Rico's cock. She felt him flinch, his body involuntarily tightening from the pleasure she gave him. Then she heard him moan, and she told herself that she mustn't give him too much pleasure too early in the day.

She had much to accomplish, but she could only do so provided Rico was desperately seeking sexual release and the only woman he wanted that release from was her.

Sometime later Svetlana heard the driver/bodyguard say, in an almost casual manner, "Señor Santiago, we'll be at the National Bank in a couple minutes. Perhaps it would be best if you got yourself . . . arranged."

"Yes," Rico replied. "Of course. You're right, of course." He chuckled "Arranged? You have a way with words."

Svetlana felt Rico grab her gently but firmly by the hair and pull her head up enough to free himself. She made a soft sound in her throat, as though to protest because she no longer had his cock in her mouth. She knew what Rico wanted to hear.

"Enough for now," he said, a gleam in his eyes as he looked at Svetlana. "Come with me to the meeting. I want to show you off." He smiled wickedly. "And then I want you to suck me until we get to the next appointment."

Svetlana looked him directly in the eyes and said, "Don't I always do what you tell me to?"

"It isn't like you have a choice," he said.

I'm so going to enjoy destroying you.

"You promise it won't be long before we're in the car again?" Svetlana asked. Her voice was soft, provocatively seductive.

"I never make promises to women," Rico said.

Oh, I'm really fucking really going to take you down hard.

Svetlana smiled at him and giggled in an almost little-girl fashion when he had to struggle to tuck his hard cock back into his trousers before zipping up. She was quite pleased with her acting ability. Rico had no idea how much she hated him.

After a rocky start to the morning, everything was now seemingly going according to plan. Svetlana inhaled deeply and breathed a sigh of relief.

"Be nice and polite, but don't say too much," Rico said. He was holding Svetlana by the arm, just above her elbow.

The instant the words were out of his mouth, Rico knew that he had royally pissed off Svetlana. She wasn't the kind of woman to be told to keep her mouth shut.

They were just about to walk into the office of the CEO of National Bank. Rico was accustomed to having a social inferior on his arm and needing to instruct her on how she was to behave when she was with her betters.

But Svetlana wasn't in that class. She didn't need anyone to teach her how to behave with society's elites. He suspected she looked down on most of the people in the upper crust of society.

In fact, she could probably give a lesson or two on how to behave properly and show the right kind of *savoir-faire*. When he realized this, his desire for her skyrocketed.

"I'm sorry," Rico said as she stepped into the boardroom. He felt a warm flush go through him. It wasn't often that he was with women who could make him feel uneasy. He much preferred it the other way around. And he never apologized for his behavior.

Svetlana stopped, looked into his eyes, and whispered, "You're just not used to getting blow jobs from someone who could say *no* to you." She blew him a kiss. Then she winked like a high school girl at a sock hop. "If you want to put your cock in my mouth again, you'd better figure that out." Her eyes suddenly turned cold as ice. "I really dislike being condescended to by any man who expects me to swallow his cum. Understand?"

Rico could hardly believe his own ears when he heard himself say, "Yes."

Rico did not know what more to say. He'd never met any woman as bold and audacious as Svetlana. And the most amazing thing of all was that she didn't want money. She had plenty of her own.

"Don't worry, I'll know what to do," Svetlana said, then slipped her hand inside Rico's as they entered the office. "We'll play this one out however you want. You're the one in charge."

So far, the meeting had been going pretty much as planned. The Chief Executive Officer of the National Bank had put forward the facts and figures that Rico had asked for, and always asked for, during their meetings, which occurred once every two weeks.

Sitting at the CEO's desk, in his chair, Rico was comfortably in charge.

Then Rico asked about the interest payments that were supposed to come from the illegal, under-the-table loans to the Columbian drug dealer who had found himself short of cash when three of his boats got stopped by Mexican authorities.

"They haven't paid the interest yet for this month," the CEO said.

"Why not?" Rico's tone was neutral, but he kept the look in his eyes cold and murderous. "There is no excuse for not making payments on time."

"He said that the authorities had been particularly vigilant lately," the CEO replied. "First they stopped and confiscated his shipment. And then they stopped one of his ships and stole more than six million dollars of his cash. He's been bled dry by the Mexican authorities." He shook his head. "The government are bigger thieves than we are."

Rico sighed wearily, as though he was speaking with a misbehaving child in high school. He looked to his left, at Svetlana, and she appeared as lovely to him as ever. To look at her sitting calmly in the chair, it was hard to remember how wanton she could be.

When her gaze met his, she smiled and said, "Do you mind if I get a little sun? It's such a beautiful day."

"Of course not, my dear," Rico replied. "Make yourself comfortable. We've still got about thirty or forty minutes before this meeting is over."

Rico made a point of not watching too closely as Svetlana rose from her chair and walked across the office to the east-facing bank of windows.

"This is such a lovely office," she said quietly as she slipped off her jacket and let it slide down her arms. When she took it off, she tossed it casually onto the floor, as though it actually wasn't a garment worth hundreds of dollars. While still looking out the window at Mexico City, she began unbuttoning her blouse. "I like being up high. I like being up near the clouds and looking down at a city."

As Svetlana unfastened the buttons of her blouse, Rico did all he could to completely ignore her, as though what she was doing was commonplace in his life. Nothing could be farther from the truth, but Rico didn't want the bank's CEO to know that.

"When will you be collecting the interest payment?" Rico asked the CEO. There was a distinct edge in his voice when he asked the question. The CEO looked at him, then looked back at Svetlana as she slipped her blouse off her shoulders, exposing herself in a demi-bra lovingly holding full breasts with nipples that were partially erect.

She likes this game.

Rico felt himself becoming erect, and he struggled to find the self-discipline to keep from throwing Svetlana to the floor, and ravaging her right then and there.

It's going to be a long day. Let's drag this out, not rush to the finish line. He looked at the CEO, who was watching as Svetlana reached between the cups to unclasp the hook-and-eye closure of her brassiere.

"Are you paying attention?" Rico asked sharply.

"Yes," the CEO replied. "Um, yes, señor." He was visibly shaken.

Rico gave him a small smile and said, slightly under his breath, "She can be distracting, can't she?"

"That's possibly the understatement of all time."

Together they watched as Svetlana removed her skirt, and then her panties, until all that she was wearing were the garter belt, stockings, and the stilettos she'd put on that morning, which in color were a perfect match for skirt-suit.

"Before you recline," Rico said, with only a hint of strain in his tone, "would you mind pouring some coffee for us? You know how I'm addicted to the stuff."

"Of course, darling," Svetlana replied. "You know I'll do whatever you want." Wantonly undressed, she crossed the room. She picked up the insulated coffee carafe and, as though a waitress wearing a cheap polyester uniform instead of only lacy lingerie, walked to the bank's CEO and filled his cup, then walked around the desk and filled Rico's cup.

"Thank you," the CEO said after several seconds. "That's very kind of you." The stress he felt was evident in his tone.

"It's my pleasure," Svetlana said, as though she wasn't, in fact, exposing herself to a complete stranger. Looking at Rico, she asked, "Is there anything else you'd like me to do?"

She had voiced the statement as though it was entirely innocent, though everyone in the room knew that innocence was not her intention. Quite the opposite, in fact.

For several seconds it seemed as though the banker was going to say something, but though his lips moved, not a word was spoken.

"Thank you, but that will be all," Rico said.

He watched, impressed beyond belief, as Svetlana returned the coffee carafe to its place on the cart, then went back to her spot in front of the window. She eased off her high-heeled shoes, then stockings, rolling them down her legs. Lastly, she removed her garter belt, then lay on her back on the carpet in the sunshine. There was nothing about her demeanor that wasn't calm, nothing that would suggest in any way that she wasn't utterly at ease being naked in a room with two men, one of whom she had just met only minutes earlier.

As Svetlana stretched out on the floor of the office of one of the most influential bankers in Mexico, Rico turned to the CEO and asked acidly, "Can I have your attention now?"

Rico was quite pleased with himself, and with Svetlana, when the CEO said, "Yes. Of course, señor." And then, after a moment of hesitation, he added, "Of course, señor. You know I'll do whatever it is you ask of me."

"Darling, do you mind if I put my clothes back on?"

Svetlana kept her tone deferential. She'd been lying on the carpeted floor for the past thirty minutes, completely naked but listening to everything that Rico and the bank's CEO were saying. They almost always spoke in Spanish, and they assumed that Svetlana didn't understand all that they were saying, but for the most part, she did. She had learned that Rico not only owned significant portion of the bank under-the-table, he was also laundering much of his drug money through it, as well as skimming profits from other drug dealers who thought the bank was doing nothing other than laundering their ill-gotten gain.

"Of course," Rico said, reacting as though she really wasn't naked. "We're finishing up here."

Svetlana slipped her bare feet into the leg holes of her panties and shimmied the bikini garment up her legs, then over the curve of her hips. She was facing the men as she did this, and she could feel the heat of their desires.

Rico is going to fuck me, and it's going to be a rough one.

It was a coldly logical awareness of what she knew was going to happen. She had toyed with his libido, and she had taunted his desires . . . but she knew that she had pushed a proud and arrogant man as far as she could, and she would now face the consequences of her behavior.

Svetlana dressed slowly, and she was consciously aware of the fact that she wasn't just putting her clothes back on, she was performing a reverse strip tease, giving a show to the two men in the room. She pretended that she wasn't aware of them looking at her, but she could feel the heat of their lust for her. Being watched excited her.

All she had to do was give the slightest inkling and they would attack like wolves rushing in for the kill. The fangs would come out. Blood would be spilled. In the very least, she'd get royally fucked.

When her clothes were all on and properly arranged, she took from her purse a small, compact mirror. Very slowly, sensually, she reapplied her lipstick. She knew every move she made was being watched. She behaved as though she had not been—just minutes earlier—completely naked in front of them. The exhibitionist in her was screaming for attention, but everything else about her was saying *shut up.*

"About finished?" she asked Rico when she had completed with her performance.

His voice was tight, taut, when he replied, "Yes."

"Then we're on our way," she said. She turned to the CEO and said, "Thank you for letting me get some sun. I hope to see you again sometime soon."

He nodded, but didn't say anything. Svetlana suspected he couldn't speak a word, even if he could figure out what he wanted to say.

CHAPTER TEN

I don't fucking care how pissed off my brother's going to be. Tomas looked at his wristwatch. It was gold, and cost more than most people in Mexico City made in a dozen years. The diamond ring on his little finger was just slightly over two carats, and its cut was considered flawless.

He resisted the urge to tell his driver to speed up. Getting in an accident wouldn't do him any good.

He looked at his fancy wristwatch again. It was just under ten minutes before his brother was expected at the Diego Construction Company. The truth of it was that Tomas couldn't care less about the millions of pesos he would make from the company and its lucrative contract with both the city of Mexico City, and the Mexican government. What he really wanted was to once again be in Svetlana's company.

There wasn't anything about her that didn't trigger every sensual receptor in Tomas's body.

I wonder if she swallows? It was a discordant thought that seemed to come into his head out of nowhere.

No, she doesn't. Women that beautiful never swallow.

Maybe if I paid her she would.

The instant this thought went through his brain, he discounted it. Women in Svetlana's economic bracket didn't do anything they didn't want to, and money would never be a deciding factor. A woman that rich couldn't be bought and sold like a chamber maid. Besides, with chamber maids he never reached for his wallet when his fists would do the trick, and do it without costing him the price of a burrito.

He touched the intercom button on the car's center console and said, "I don't want to be late."

"We'll be there on time," the driver/bodyguard replied without a moment's hesitation.

Will she scream if I fuck her in the ass?

It was a tempting, devilish thought for Tomas to consider. If he fucked Svetlana in the ass, and she started to cry . . . it wouldn't be the first time he'd fucked a crying women. He smiled. A woman crying made his cock harder, his lust hotter.

This is a day with potential. I just hope her father doesn't go all psycho when his little girl gets nailed by me and Rico at the same time.

What the fuck is he doing here?

But the instant the thought went through his brain, Rico knew what the answer was. His brother had shown up at the Diego Construction Company because Svetlana was in the SUV with him, and Tomas wasn't one to allow himself to be left out of the action. Not when the woman was that gorgeous.

"Were you followed?" Rico asked, standing outside his SUV.

Tomas shook his head. "Of course not. Our men are always careful."

"In that case, it's good to see you," Rico said to his brother. "I guess you cancelled your other meetings?"

Tomas nodded. "They weren't that important."

Like fuck they weren't, you liar.

"Señor Diego will be pleased that both of us have shown up for this meeting," Rico said diplomatically. "He likes it when we show him respect."

"Actually, he's an arrogant prick, and I pretty much loathe him, but that's not really the issue this afternoon, now is it?"

Rico watched as his kid brother looked inside the SUV at Svetlana, then back and him. He could feel the sexual energy emanating from his brother. How many times had they shared a woman? Dozens, to be sure. But Svetlana seemed to be different from the other women and girls. He couldn't exactly say why—it wasn't just that she was extraordinarily beautiful—but he could tell that she was different.

And it wasn't just that she had money, though that certainly was an enormous difference.

Rico looked at his wristwatch, saw the time, and announced, "We'd better get in there. Our meeting's scheduled to begin right now."

I'm going to get fucked.

It wasn't exactly an epiphany for Svetlana, but when she looked into Tomas's eyes and saw the lusty intensity there, she knew with certainty that the odds of her keeping her panties on were almost nil.

"We'd better hurry," Svetlana said. "We don't want to be late."

Rico said, "Señor Diego will wait until I tell him he doesn't have to any longer. Trust me on this one. He'll wait until I tell him otherwise."

Svetlana could feel the tension between the brothers. She knew that both of them wanted to have sex with her. Of that singular fact, she had no doubts whatsoever. But there was something else, a sharp, serrated edge of emotion between them that she couldn't quite put properly into place in her mind.

They loved each other. But just beneath the surface of that love was a competitiveness and a resentment that went down to the marrow of the bone.

They loved each other as close brothers, but they despised each other as competitive siblings.

Cain and Abel didn't harbor this much hatred in their hearts.

They walked into the construction company with Rico leading the way. When they were ushered into the president's office, he immediately got out of his chair and walked toward them with his hand extended and his smile broad and effusive.

"It's so good to see you again," he said.

Svetlana watched as they shook hands, but she could sense the undercurrent of tension and fear in the company president's soul. He was scared of the Santiago brothers, and Svetlana suspected that most sane people would be. She was scared of them, and wouldn't be ashamed to admit it.

Rico sat behind the desk in the president's chair. There were two chairs facing the desk. Svetlana, understanding her place in the hierarchy, walked to the windows and looked out. No one made a move to get her a chair.

"It's an honor to have both of you here," the president said. "And I see you've brought a friend. I feel honored."

"Yes," Rico said. "This is Svetlana, and she is most definitely a friend."

Svetlana suppressed a smile. She'd had many titles during her time with Omega Force, but never *friend.*

"It's good to meet you," Svetlana said, then turned back to the window.

Rico was looking at the computer monitor, nodding his head slightly as though approving whatever was on the screen.

"I've printed out everything you've got on the computer so we can go through the records together," the president said, and once again Svetlana could hear the stress in his voice. "I think you're going to be pleased with the progress we've made since your last visit."

As Svetlana looked out the large window at Mexico City, the men began talking business, and though she gave the appearance of being entirely disinterested, her attention was entirely focused on what the men were saying.

She learned that there was a construction project underway at the northwest corner of the city which would provide office space for small, commercial businesses that was coming along very nicely, both on schedule and budget. But if there should be delays—say, closer to the completion date—then the cost overruns would be highly profitable and seem entirely legitimate. It was Rico's opinion that the delays should start no earlier than thirty days prior to the deadline. Tomas concurred.

"Svetlana, can you come a little closer?" Rico asked without taking his eyes off the computer monitor.

She knew his tone was casual but his intent was not. Nothing that Rico ever did was innocent.

She walked across the office until she was at his side. He never acknowledged her presence. He didn't even look away from his monitor even once. With his right hand he reached out and slipped it around Svetlana's leg, just above her knee. Svetlana inhaled through her nostrils quickly and deeply, but other than that, she did nothing to keep him from touching her.

"This record here for managerial overtime," Rico said, his eyes narrowing ominously, "seems a bit suspicious to me. I can understand overtime pay for the construction workers, but not for their managers."

"It's all quite legitimate, I assure you," the president said quickly, his tone defensive. "They've been working like slaves to stay on schedule and on budget."

"Then work like slaves without getting overtime," Rico said coldly. "They're making one hell of a lot more than the men working construction."

Svetlana said quietly, "Your heart is always on the side of the little guy, isn't it?" She didn't mean it, since she knew better regarding Rico, but she also knew what it was he wanted to hear.

"Always," Rico replied, finally looking away from the monitor and gave her a smile. She was only a little surprised that it was an honest smile. "I'll never forget my roots. I'll always remember where I started."

Self-righteous, murderous bastard. You'd kill a blind beggar if he had coins in his tin cup.

Svetlana inhaled sharply once again when Rico simultaneously turned his attention back to the monitor and the facts and figures on display there and slid the palm of his right hand up the inside of her thigh, pushing her dress up as he did so. Svetlana flinched, but other than that she did not move, and she knew him well enough to not protest what was being done to her.

"I'll want a more complete breakdown of those overtime expenses for management," Rico said.

He slid his hand higher, up to the top of Svetlana's thigh, above her stocking top, lingered there for a while, then went higher still, until he cupped the cheek of her ass, caressing her lightly, casually through her bikini panties. His touch was firm and confident.

Though there was a desk between Rico and the president and Svetlana, now that his hand was on her ass, they could undoubtedly guess what he was doing to her. Svetlana stood quietly, her hands together in front of her, feeling the strong fingers kneading her bottom.

"And look down three cells," Rico said, as though he wasn't really feeling the ass of a beautiful woman while studying an excel spreadsheet, "there's something marked *ancillary supplies*." He shook his head and gave Svetlana's bottom a squeeze. "Whatever the hell that is, I don't like it. Even if it is legitimate, you've got to give me more information than that if you expect me to not dock it out of your personal pay."

The breath hitched in Svetlana's chest when Rico eased his hand under the leg hole of her panties and began caressing her ass without the barrier of cotton separating his touch from her body. What was going on, she knew, was a power play, with Rico intimately touching her in front of the company president and his brother just so that he could show them how much control he had over the people in his life. And he probably wanted to humiliate her, at least a little, especially since he now knew she came from a wealthy family. Humiliating women was like caviar for the libido to men like Rico. It was to be experienced slowly, savored leisurely, like a connoisseur, not gulped like a glutton.

Intimidating an impoverished woman was easy, and it proved almost nothing about a man's power. But controlling a woman who was worth millions — if not, in fact, billions — was something that the president would be impressed with. So would Tomas.

Though Svetlana would never admit it, she was getting excited by being groped by Rico while two other men watched. The exhibitionist in Svetlana's libido could not be entirely ignored, no matter how much she wanted to turn a blind eye.

Besides, nothing truly bad would happen in this office. In the limousine, it would be different. But here, in front of the construction company president, there were boundaries that she felt the Santiago brothers wouldn't cross.

And as she felt her pussy getting warmer, becoming creamy, she found that it was increasingly difficult to concentrate on the very important business issues that were being discussed.

Don't touch my pussy. Please, don't touch my pussy.

She was relieved — well, almost, anyway — when Rico eased his hand out from under her panties and began stroking his palm up and down on her inner thigh, over her silk stocking. Svetlana felt the tingles going through her body, the hand caressing her entirely arousing, especially when there was an audience of two so nearby. Her clit began to throb, very softly at first, but she knew that over time the sensation would grow stronger and stronger.

In many ways, her body was a traitor to her best instincts.

Rico had another question for the company president, but the buzzing in Svetlana's ears was so strong that she could not hear what the words were.

For a moment—just a second or two—she let her gaze go up from the desktop to the men sitting across the desk. Both Tomas and the president were watching with an eagle's eye the way the back of her dress lifted and lowered as Rico stroked her leg and bottom slowly, casually, and illicitly.

"You *are* paying attention," Rico said to the president, his tone caustic. "Aren't you?"

Svetlana looked at the man. He was staring at her—or, more accurately, staring at where the hand must be under her dress.

Speak, you damned fool.

As though coming out of a trance, the president gave his head a little shake, and then said, "Yes. Of course, Señor Santiago. And once again, can I say that I'm honored that both you and your brother have decided to come see me at the same time?"

They do other things together, and at the same time.

It was a caustic, dangerous thought, and Svetlana immediately banished it from her memory—or at least tried to. The brothers were men who killed people if they thought they had been disrespected, and they ordered those murders without hesitation or remorse.

Rico's attention did not waver from the monitor as his hand eased up the inside of Svetlana's thigh. But this time he didn't stop at the top of her thigh. This time the side of his index finger pressed against her pussy, touching her through her panties.

Svetlana could not stifle the soft gasp that came from her, and when she eventually resumed breathing, she took in air through slightly parted lips.

"And if you look at column *B* you'll see another issue I

have," Rico said, an edge in his voice as his finger slid back and forth over the entrance to Svetlana's pussy, touching her through her panties. His touch was firm but deft.

"Column *B*, you say?" the president replied, having to turn his attention away from Svetlana and back to the printed pages on a clipboard in his hand.

My panties are getting wet, and Rico's going to feel that. Damn. A thousand times damn.

It took some discipline, but Svetlana was able to keep her eyes open, though cast downward, as Rico rubbed the side of his finger back and forth over the lips of her pussy.

At least he's not touching my clit.

A moment later she cursed herself for the thought, because almost instantly, Rico's caresses shifted forward and slightly upward, and when he moved his hand, he was creating friction against her clit in a most utterly taboo, enticing way.

It was as though he could read her mind . . . and her deepest fears.

"And regarding the increase in the price of concrete, I'd like to have a more detailed explanation for that," Rico said, as he put a bit more pressure behind his fingers while touching Svetlana firmly, intimately through her panties. "It's not that I doubt your accounting, mind you, it's just that I need to know what I'm paying for."

No one in the room believed what he was saying, and Svetlana knew it. He was just proving — to her, and the men in the room — that he had ultimate power, and unless he was shown the proper respect, then penalties would be meted out. The sole judge and jury to make decisions on these orders would be Rico — and no one else. And there would be no appeal.

Then, without notice, Rico took his hand out from beneath Svetlana's skirt, and he stopped touching her so wickedly.

Svetlana knew in her rational brain that she should be happy, but her erotic receptors were giving her quite a different message. She wanted Rico to touch her as much as she didn't want him to. The dichotomy made her dizzy.

"I have to use the restroom, so this meeting is adjourned until I come back," Rico said. And then, as he made his way to the office door, he muttered, "I just drink too damned much coffee. Makes me have to pee all the time."

Tomas and the president chuckled softly at the joke.

Now that she was standing alone without a hand up her skirt, Svetlana felt entirely disoriented. Going from being intimately caressed while two men she hardly knew at all watched it happening to standing alone and being untouched was emotionally jolting. Her libido was screaming *What the fuck?*

When I take these men down, I'm not going to feel an ounce of regret. Whatever shitty thing happens to them, they deserve it.

She smiled inside, though she didn't let it show in her expression. But the thought — the *awareness* — did make her feel better. Sometimes her emotions could get distracted from the mission, but never long. She was too seasoned of a professional secret agent for her to ever forget just who she was, and what her mission was.

But sometimes her emotions and thoughts strayed.

Tomas cleared his throat to draw attention to himself. When Svetlana looked at him, he smiled at her, and when he did, a shiver of horror went through Svetlana. Rico was deadly and cruel, she knew — but Tomas was worse. Tomas was handsome to the point of almost being beautiful, but when Svetlana looked into his eyes, she couldn't see a soul. She could see malevolence and greed and lust and sadism. Those traits were all readily apparent. But she couldn't see a soul.

And that frightened her to the marrow of her bones, because she had only seen it in men a handful of times, and every time she'd seen it, she knew that she was looking at the very essence of sophisticated evil.

"Svetlana, please come a little closer," Tomas said, his tone the essence of charm while his intention the embodiment of evil. "These business meetings can be a little boring, and I think if you were to sit on my lap, I'd have something to help me focus."

Do you really think calling me a thing *is going to warm me up to you?*

Svetlana had just discovered which one of the brothers she loathed the most.

Why is it the magnificently gorgeous ones who are always the worst bastards?

Svetlana decided that was a question for someone above her pay grade, then shrugged it off as she walked around the desk and stepped up to Tomas. She knew she had no choice but to yield to whatever Tomas's wishes were, and in a way, that made her actions easier. She reminded herself what her mission was.

"Are you having a good time with us today?" Tomas asked.

He'd asked the question as though defying Svetlana to say she wasn't. *The gods can be cruel.*

"Of course," she said. But then, a couple seconds later, and with a slight bite in her tone, she added, "Why wouldn't I?"

She saws a flicker of anger glint in his eyes, and she knew she had made her sarcastic point, and that he'd understood it.

"Come closer," Tomas said quietly, malevolently. "Sit on my lap."

Before Svetlana could follow the command that she had been given—and she had no illusion that it was anything other than a command—Rico walked back into the office.

"Now where were we?" he said as he returned to the president's chair. "Oh, yes. The Sullivan Project." He smiled at Svetlana, then at the men in the room. "That's a pet project of mine. I thought it up, crammed the damned thing through the bureaucracy, and made sure that all the licenses and permits got signed." He looked Svetlana directly in the eyes. "It's for low-income housing. It's so that people who don't make a lot of money can still have a place to live and have a family with a roof over their heads." His smile broadened. "I try to do a lot regarding low income housing. And when the cost over-runs come in, I'll make millions. Simply millions."

CHAPTER ELEVEN

I've never met a more sanctimonious bastard in my life. And if there's a woman who knows a posturing prick when she sees one, it's me — because I've seen so many in my life I can't damned stand it.

"Over here," Tomas said, patting his thigh. He kept his tone low, but authoritarian. "Let's let the meeting continue." He looked at his brother. "Once again, where were we?"

"The Sullivan Project."

"Oh, yes." A moment later, when Svetlana was about to sit on his on his lap with her back toward the president, Tomas turned her around so she faced him.

She sat down and put an arm around his shoulders, leaving her other hand in her lap.

"You've always been pleased with that one. I heard, though, that there were issues with the quality of steel that was being used."

Tomas put his hand on Svetlana's knee, touching her through her stocking.

It took some effort for her to look away from the hand on her leg, her gaze moving over the desk and up to Rico's face as he studied the monitor.

"The steel came from China," the president said. "It was very cheap, but when we realized it wasn't up to code, we went with an American competitor."

"Has the inferior steel been removed?"

"No, sir. We used what we had, and then we made the switch."

Tomas smiled and nodded as his right hand eased slowly up Svetlana's leg, pushing her skirt higher and higher.

Now she understood why Tomas had turned her around. It was so the president could see what was being done to her.

She wanted to grab him by the wrist and stop him, but she knew that to deny Tomas's wishes was to court disaster.

When his hand reached the top of her stocking, he stopped. With his thumb, he caressed bare skin, and with his fingers, he fondled her through her silk stocking. As he did this, he never turned his attention away from his brother.

"Nice move," Tomas said to the president. "No wasted money, no wasted steel. I like the way you think."

The president dragged his gaze up from Svetlana's thigh to Tomas's face. "Thank you, señor," he said. "I'm glad you approve."

Svetlana exhaled slowly, with relief, when she felt Tomas's hand slide down all the way to her knee.

It was the casual cruelty of what was being done to her that was so infuriating. But there was also an illicit quality to the moment—forbidden, exhibitionistic, coerced—that held within it elements of eroticism which Svetlana couldn't deny. Tomas began stroking his fingertips lightly from her knee to the top of her thigh, and as he did this, he never turned his attention away from Rico. There was something terribly erotic about being caressed by a man who did it so cavalierly.

Oh, no . . . I'm getting wet . . . again. It was about the last thing she wanted.

Svetlana knew he was going to touch her pussy. A man like Tomas wouldn't tolerate a woman as vulnerable as Svetlana was at that moment without taking full advantage of the situation. She was certain of it . . . and even anticipated it. Though she wished she didn't.

But he didn't. Instead, he took the hem of her skirt between his forefinger and thumb and almost gently pulled the garment down to cover her thighs properly.

Svetlana could hear the buzzing in her brain. Every time she thought she knew the Santiago brothers, they did something that she hadn't even considered was a possibility.

No wonder the authorities can't get anything on them. It's like a chess game, and they're always two or three moves ahead of the good guys.

Tomas turned his head and looked up into Svetlana's eyes. He gave her a handsome smile, and the dimple in his cheek appeared. Svetlana understood how so many women would completely fall under his spell.

In a whisper, he said, "You're so pretty." He reached up and lightly stroked her cheek with the pads of his fingers. "I'll bet men have been telling you that since you were a little girl."

Only creepy men. And I was a little girl.

"They have . . . but I very seldom believed them." She cleared her throat. "Men who say that to little girls aren't the kind of men to be believed."

"You should." His fingertips went from her temple down to her cheek, then to her throat. "Every one of them was speaking the truth."

Don't caress my throat. Please, please don't. I've got the most sensitive throat in the world. I'd have been a virgin a lot longer than I was if a boy hadn't started kissing me on the neck.

Sternly, Rico asked, "Are you paying attention, Tomas? We're not disturbing you with this business meeting, are we?"

Tomas looked at his brother, smiled charmingly — because every time he smiled it was charming — and replied, "No. Of course not. You were talking about whether or not we should put up a security fence around the Sullivan property so that equipment won't get stolen." His right hand eased downward from Svetlana's throat. "I think that's a good idea, especially since we're going to be bringing in the next shipment of lumber. Maybe some guards on the property wouldn't be such a bad idea."

Svetlana watched as Rico's eyes narrowed, and then widened as he smiled. "I like that idea."

The fingers of Tomas's right hand eased down between the halves of her blouse to where the top button was fastened. While still looking at Rico, his fingers eased the top button out through the hole.

Svetlana felt her heart go from a canter to flat-out galloping. A second, third, and then fourth button was unfastened with effortless skill.

Still without looking at her, Tomas eased her blouse open, sliding the silk around her breasts to expose her lovely pink demi-bra. The closure of her bra was between the cups, and when Tomas touched it, Svetlana put her left hand on his. She didn't grab his hand, she simply touched the back of it lightly with her fingertips.

When he turned his attention away from Rico and looked up at her, Svetlana saw in the dark depths of his eyes something akin to a murderous, raw fury. This was not a man who would allow any woman to decide the circumstances under which he could touch her.

It was a frightening awareness, and it reminded her of just exactly what kind of men she was dealing with in the Santiago brothers.

Tomas took Svetlana's hand in his, curling his fingers around it. When his fingers tightened, he did it strongly enough to cause discomfort. It wasn't quite pain, but it was on the threshold. The threat was there. Then, slowly and deliberately, he moved her left hand until it was behind her back, then he grabbed her by the wrist with his hand that had been behind her.

In a somewhat strained voice, Rico said, "Tomas, as long as it's all right with you, I'll continue."

With an uncompromising expression on his face, Tomas

answered, "Please. Don't let me hold things up. Just had a . . . situation . . . that I had to deal with." He smiled. "Everything is fine now."

The fingers around her left wrist were like a steel band biting into her flesh. She wanted to say it wasn't necessary to hold her so tightly, but she knew that the slightest complaint would be considered a full-frontal act of defiance. A reprisal for defiance would be swift and severe. Svetlana had no doubts about that.

Rico said, "How are the culverts coming for the waterway?"

The president cleared his throat behind his fist before answering. He was having a difficult time keeping his eyes off Svetlana, especially now that her blouse was completely unbuttoned and opened.

"It's on time and on budget," the president said. "We'll be bringing water to the heart of the city, where it is needed the most, in less than four months. The pipeline will bring clean water to millions of people who have never had clean water in their lives."

As Tomas used one hand to unclasp the closure of Svetlana's bra, she was looking into Rico's eyes. His dark eyes were bright and alive.

"People who have never had clean, fresh water will now have it. And all because of the Santiago brothers. What do you think of that?"

Tomas had unfastened her bra, and the moment he did, the twin cups fell away from her breasts, exposing her mounds. Despite her best intentions to remain utterly silent, Svetlana gasped softly, and all three men in the room uttered a short, masculine sigh.

"Well?" Rico prodded. "What do you think of that?"

He needs homage and adulation the way a junkie needs his needle.

"I think the people of Mexico City have been blessed to

have Rico and Tomas Santiago among their citizens."

I also think you're going to have a lot to answer for when you meet your Maker.

The buzzing in her ears grew even louder when Tomas began to casually squeeze and fondle her now naked breasts. He would caress one breast, and then the other, all while seemingly paying no attention whatsoever to what his hand was doing. Occasionally he would take a nipple between finger and thumb, and when he did, he would pinch with more force than was necessary, and he would twist the nipple with such strength that Svetlana would clench her teeth to keep from making so much as a single sound of protest. She knew that to protest was to invite more of the same.

This situation could have had erotic elements to it, but with Tomas almost constantly using more force than was ideal, at this moment what was being done to her was nothing more than an unpleasant experience that Svetlana had to endure for Omega Force and her country.

"You don't foresee any problems with the culvert?" Rico asked the president.

Svetlana was not sure whether the president responded to the question, because in the next moment Tomas had stopped tormenting her nipples, and had chosen instead to suck lightly, even gently, upon them.

He's a bastard . . . but that feels really nice.

To go from nearly wanting to scream because of the pain Tomas was inflicting upon her, then feel like moaning because of the soothing and satisfying pleasure his lips and tongue gave to her nipples, was an emotional boomerang for Svetlana that left her feeling disoriented. She tried to grasp reality in her hands, but it was like trying to grab a handful of smoke.

"You are listening, aren't you?" Rico asked.

Tomas was, at that precise moment, sucking on Svetlana's left nipple. Tomas straightened his spine, and in doing so, extricated Svetlana's nipple from his mouth with a rather pronounced slurping sound. The sound of it seemed to amuse him.

"Yes, I'm listening." He grinned lewdly. "I'm multi-tasking."

To Svetlana, Rico asked, "You're not finding our business meetings too boring?"

Now that she was no longer being tormented, it was easier for her to lie. "No, of course not. What could be more interesting than sitting in on a discussion about culverts to provide fresh water to people who have never had fresh water in their lives?"

The painful throbbing in her nipples was diminishing rapidly.

She saw the look of surprise on Rico's face. "So you have been paying attention. I'm impressed." He pushed his chair a little ways away from the desk. "Please come here, Svetlana."

Tomas released the hold he had on her wrist immediately. By doing so, he informed Svetlana that Rico was the Alpha male between them, and there was no doubt about who held all the power in his hands, and who was just a pretender to the throne. They had the same last name, but they certainly didn't have the same power.

"Sit on my lap, my darling," Rico said, his voice smooth and without stress. "My brother seems to have come up with a very good idea, but I see no reason why he shouldn't share."

Svetlana sat on Rico's thigh, and he immediately began sucking on her nipples. The pretense of having a business meeting was temporarily abandoned as Rico feasted on Svetlana's bosom. As he suckled, she looked over the desk at Tomas and the company's president.

She realized that she was in a room with three men who had great power, and virtually no ability to control themselves in the use of that power. She couldn't imagine a worse combination than power without self-discipline.

You think you're strong, but the fact is, you'll do anything necessary — move mountains if that's what it takes — to get sexual satisfaction. You're not strong. I'm the one who has the power.

She looked down at Rico, who was sucking on her right nipple as he squeezed her left breast.

"You do that just right," she said softly. She stroked her fingers over his close-cropped, ebony black hair. "You make me wet when you do that to me."

Svetlana heard Tomas's sharp inhalation, and she knew she had offended him — which she hadn't intended to do, but now that she realized she had, she had every intention of twisting the knife. If she could create a fissure between the brothers, cause them to start fighting between themselves, then so much the better. The more they hated each other, the less power they had. It truly was just as simple as that.

"That's it," Svetlana purred, taking Rico's face in both hands and guiding him to the crest of her other breast. "Yes, yes, yes . . . just like that. That's perfect." She lifted his face, then dipped down to kiss him. When their lips met, Svetlana made a point of kissing Rico in such a manner that both the president and Tomas could see her tongue. She was twisting the knife in Tomas's guts as hard as she could. She knew it, and she liked doing it, because he was the man who had caused such things to happen. Pulling back only slightly, with her lips still touching Rico's, she said loud enough so that everyone in the room could hear her, "I'll bet you could make me come just by kissing me."

The smoke's got to be coming out of Tomas's ears by now. She hoped this was true. She wanted Tomas in torment.

Svetlana wanted to look at Tomas. She wanted to confirm that he was furious with all the flattering things that she had just been saying about his arch-rival, who also happened to be his older brother.

But she didn't dare. She wasn't sure she was a good

enough actress. Maybe he'd see in her eyes that she was intentionally belittling him, that she was saying the words that she knew would pit one Santiago brother against another. And the instant he knew she was playing him for the fool, he'd be on his guard.

And a man like Tomas Santiago would unleash the forces of hell on anyone who played him for the sucker. Even if she had pretty eyes and a pliable libido.

Looking into Rico's eyes, with her face just inches from his, Svetlana said, "As lovely as this interlude is, don't you think you should get back to the meeting? Once we're finished, it's back to the limo. And you know what fancy cars do to my sex drive, darling."

For a full five minutes, Rico seemed to be completely concentrating on nothing other than the Excel spreadsheet on his computer, even though he had a beautiful blonde on his lap, with her blouse unbuttoned and her bra opened, with both of her breasts glistening with his saliva because he had been sucking on them. Svetlana occasionally stroked her palm over his head, and sometimes she shifted her weight slightly, to add or reduce some pressure to the erection he had trapped inside his trousers, which pressed against her, but other than that, she sat quietly, even subserviently, on his lap.

She could almost feel the heat radiating from Tomas's forehead. She had not been the perfect subservient with him, she hadn't willingly accepted her role as sex-slave to him. But for Rico she had done precisely that, and Svetlana could tell she had forced the younger brother to swallow a bitter, poisonous pill. He was Number Two, and every move Svetlana made said precisely that.

If I play this right, maybe I'll get these two pricks to kill each other, and save Omega Force the necessary task of doing it to make the world a better place.

Svetlana discovered, now that she knew the brothers were displeased with each other if not in fact feuding, she was able to take a bit more sensual pleasure about what was being done to her body, without feeling the slightest bit of anxiety or guilt because of it.

I'd have sex with the devil in front of both of them, if it fucked with their psyches.

The thought made her smile, and very nearly made her laugh. Because of her reaction, she had to pretend that her joyous mood was caused by Rico's exquisite sensual skills. Svetlana was a woman who had to pretend very often.

But Svetlana's sense of victory came to a quick end when Rico brought his hand from her breast, and reached between her thighs.

Don't. Don't. Not there.

"So how many action items do we have left?" Rico asked, looking at the company president as his hand slid up Svetlana's thigh, over her silk stockings, inching closer and closer to panties that had become damp. "I'm finding myself becoming increasingly interested in seeing this meeting come to a conclusion."

Svetlana inhaled sharply when Rico fingers touched her intimately through her panties. There wasn't a nerve in her cunt that wasn't on high alert.

When she looked over at Tomas, his face was red with fury.

If it takes getting touched like this to make the brothers hate each other, then this is a very small price to pay.

There were times when Svetlana was quite pleased with her ability to properly prioritize.

CHAPTER TWELVE

"Get in the car." Tomas was standing at the door of the limousine outside the construction company. There was a prominent bulge in his trousers, and a very nasty edge in his emotions. He didn't just want to have sex, he wanted to hate-fuck. Nastily. Violently. It wasn't often he was in this mood, but Svetlana had driven him to it.

In the construction company's office, Tomas's brother had one-upped him once again. It had been Tomas who had to open Svetlana's blouse and suck on her nipples, but it was Rico who had put his hand between her legs and finger-fucked her — and did it all while looking at a computer monitor and pretending that profit and loss reports were actually important.

He looked into Svetlana's eyes. They were the bluest blue that he had ever seen. And they showed the fact that she was scared. Tomas didn't mind that. In fact, it pleased the hell out of him. He wanted her scared. He wanted her not knowing what was going to happen next. She had allowed Rico to do things to her body that she had refused him . . . and that was a sin for which Tomas intended that Svetlana would pay. And dearly.

He just didn't know what her punishment should be.

All he was really sure of was that she was guilty, she should be made to suffer . . . and that his vengeance should be very, very severe.

And he would be the one to administer that punishment.

"Ease up, brother," Rico said. He, of course, got into the

limousine first. He sat in the back seat, with the center console to his left.

"Yeah. Right." Tomas indicated Svetlana was to sit in the rearward facing seat, then he got in, leaving Svetlana to be the last to get in. "It's got to be tequila time, isn't it?"

Svetlana watched as Rico reached over the console, put his hand on his younger brother's shoulder, and gave it a firm squeeze. She could see that there was legitimate affection between the brothers, despite the unending competitiveness.

"To tell you the truth," Rico said, his voice solemn and sincere, "after that last meeting, I'm finding myself a touch on the thirsty side of life. What about both of us having a shot of tequila a little early today?"

Svetlana watched as Tomas smiled, and she suddenly got the impression that the two of them were like a knife and a sharpening stone. They rubbed each other raw, but in doing so, they made each other sharper, they honed each other to a razor's edge. Individually, they were intelligent thugs, but just thugs nevertheless. But together, they were a force the entire world had to reckon with. They were a single entity that, when combined, had the strength and force and deadliness of an army of men.

They are a thousand times more dangerous than I had first thought.

A shiver went through Svetlana. The vital importance of her mission had just been hammered home to her, and the reality of what would happen if she failed scared her to the depths of her soul. These weren't merely dangerous men, they were monsters. *You don't reason with monsters, you kill them.*

She sat and crossed her legs at the knee, making sure that she didn't give either of the Santiago brothers an upskirt view, despite what they had already done to her and what they had seen of her. Svetlana had little assurance as to what her immediate future had in store.

As though she hadn't just been fondled, caressed, kissed — on body parts more than just her mouth — Svetlana looked at the Santiago brothers and breezily asked, "So, where are we going now?"

Tomas made a growling sound in his throat, his teeth clenched, and his hands balled int fists.

For a second or two, Svetlana was not at all certain he wouldn't strike out violently with his fists. If he did, she wouldn't have been surprised.

"It's only a couple minutes to the warehouse, so there's not time for me to do to you want I really want to," Tomas said. The undercurrent of violence in his tone and words could not be ignored. "But this day is a long way from being finished."

Svetlana leaned toward Tomas and patted his knee, then gave it a squeeze. "I know that," she said, her voice soft and consoling. "But don't you worry, I'm a Russian woman, and we're never satisfied unless our men are satisfied." She looked him directly in the eyes and said, "And I promise you, when the night's over, you'll be satisfied." She chuckled. "Like never before."

Tomas leaned forward and took her by the wrist. He pulled her toward himself forcefully, literally jerking her out of the seat and dragging her onto his lap. An instant later, he was grabbing her head with both hands and pulling her face down to his, forcing her to kiss him. His tongue was immediately in her mouth. She did not protest its invasion, though she almost gagged. *He's not just his brother's younger sibling, he's his brother's vicious baby brother.*

Svetlana let him explore her mouth with his tongue. His hands moved from her face to squeeze the cheeks of her ass beneath her skirt. The kiss was harsh, brutal rather than dominating, and she came to the awful awareness that Tomas was a man who thought he was a Dominant, but in truth, he was just a bully. He didn't know the difference, but Svetlana had no doubt that the women who knew him most certainly did.

He would never know the difference, and he lacked the self-awareness to understand what it was he lacked.

If he was a better man, she would have pitied him. Instead, she just hoped that Karma would play out its cards properly, and that he got dealt exactly the hand that he deserved.

She squirmed on Tomas's lap, because she knew he wanted her to wriggle. When he thrust his fingers beneath her panties to touch her even more intimately, she did not protest. He wasn't brutal this time. It surprised her. Subtlety wasn't his forte.

"We're almost there," Rico said. There was a certain apology in his tone. "Come on, brother, this won't take long. And then when we're done, there's only one stop left, and then there's nothing to distract us."

Svetlana could feel the frustration, the suppressed violence in Tomas when he kissed her one last time, then pushed her away. She was a bit breathless, but not with passion. The closer and deeper she got into Tomas's psyche, the scarier it was for her. It was true that he was the beta sibling, but when it came to savagery, Svetlana had no doubts that he was the superior. And it wasn't just that he was willing to use violence to get what he wanted, it was that he *wanted* to use violence. Blood in the streets wasn't just the necessary price one paid to do business in Mexico City, it was the mother's milk that satisfied the thirsty soul that longed for such sustenance.

"Here we are," Rico said as the limousine began to slow, pulling into the vast yard filled with old warehouses, all of which looked like they hadn't been used in years. "Come on, Tomas, we'll make this quick, and then it'll be time for tequila and Svetlana."

Svetlana looked at Tomas, then turned her face away.

He's so beautiful . . . and he's one of the ugliest men I've ever met in my entire life.

121

When she started to get out of the limousine, Rico stopped her.

"Not this time. You stay out here. This won't take long." He gave her a smile that had no warmth in it. "Tomas will get over it as soon as he has his orgasm. Sometimes he gets in a mood. But once he has his climax, the mood goes away."

"I understand," Svetlana said.

And she did. She no longer harbored any illusions regarding men.

She had known vicious, violent men who—post-orgasmic—were actually decent men. But not until they'd had their orgasm. Pre-orgasm, they were heartless barbarians. But once their lust was satisfied, their aggression level was like that of a lamb in the pasture. It was as though they were someone else.

Svetlana watched as Rico and Tomas passed between the twin security guards who wore the uniforms of a private security firm and carried Kalashnikov rifles on leather slings. They had the look of men who had killed others in the past and wouldn't mind at all doing it again before the sun set.

Now why would they not want me to go in there, when they've been more than willing to taunt me and flaunt me to the other people they do business with? They haven't made a secret of what they do for business.

This question rattled around in Svetlana's head for a little over a minute before she knew exactly why they hadn't invited her in, when they had at the other stops.

Svetlana got out of the car, and when the driver gave her a dangerous look, she made a motion with her hand to calm him.

"I'm just calling my boyfriend. He makes me keep in touch, especially when I'm fucking around on him."

The driver grinned. Svetlana returned that grin with a smile that said she wouldn't mind fucking him. She wouldn't fuck him, but he believed she meant it, and that was all that was really important.

Standing beside the limousine's open door, she tapped into her gold-plated telephone four numbers, and when she had, she heard a soft *ping*, like that of an old-fashioned typewriter when the carriage has reached its end.

It meant that she had just sent a message to Jack Durbin, giving them the GPS location of the laboratory that the Santiago brothers were using to make their coronavirus.

Svetlana mumbled something about having mistyped in a phone number, because she knew that she was being watched.

"To hell with it," she said as she got back into the back seat of the limousine. "Is it time for cocktail hour?"

Soon I'll either find out that I was right . . . or I'll be responsible for the deaths of everyone in that warehouse, because what's about to happen is going to be really nasty. Jack and his men don't play games, and they don't take prisoners.

"We've got it," Jack said, looking at his laptop computer. There was a small blue dot pulsating on a map of Mexico City. The *ping* was in a two-meter radius of the initial signal. "She's found the lab."

Brad and Nigel were sitting nearby in the hotel room. Beside them wore backpacks laden with explosives. They were wearing the clothes of men who did not have jobs and had not made any honest money in many months. They were grimy and unwashed. They smelled of poverty and dissolution and alcohol.

"It's only eight miles from here," Jack said. "We'll take the car to within a couple blocks from there, and then we'll walk." He smiled at his men. "We're about to earn our money."

In his heart of hearts, Rico knew that it was safe to walk into the warehouse where he had highly paid scientists who specialized in viral infections. They were working day and night to find a new coronavirus to infect the Western world and kill as many of their citizens and members of the military as possible. But every time he stepped into the warehouse/laboratory, he felt his balls tighten up, and his mouth suddenly become as dry as a desert. Chemical warfare scared the living shit out of him.

It's safe.

He told himself that, but he didn't really believe it as he walked through the door and into the laboratory. He could feel himself begin to perspire.

There were waist-high plexiglass square tubes surrounding where the experiments were taking place. And every several feet there were long, arm-length rubber gloves in place attached through the plexiglass so that the scientists would not actually have to expose themselves to the bacteria. They could stand outside the tube while their gloved hands were inside it. They were creating a flu virus, which would — if all went according to plan — kill hundreds of millions of people.

Rico looked at the three scientists he had employed. They were in casual clothes. They wore T-shirts so they could easily put their hands and arms in and out of the rubber gloves. As Rico stepped into the room, all three held electronic tablets, and were studying them intently. It was as though they knew the Santiago brothers were going to show up and wanted to look busy. Rico felt his inner warning system become just a little more clamorous. He paid the scientists, but he didn't trust them. He didn't trust anyone. Not completely. Only, maybe, his brother.

"How are you progressing?" Rico asked, addressing the senior of the scientists. He was the only one who could speak both English and Spanish. "Are you still on schedule?"

"Yes, señor," the man said. He was in his late sixties, and he wore his hair in a ponytail, even though he was bald on top. It wasn't a flattering look for him. Or for any man.

"We have made significant progress," the lead scientist said. He spoke English. His accent was Eastern European, but not Russian. "What we're trying to do now is make those people who are infected contagious for at least thirty days before they show any symptoms of the virus. That way they will infect countless times more people before anyone knows anything is wrong. The rate of viral infection will go up exponentially if they can transmit the disease without showing any signs of it."

Despite his misgivings and anxiety about being in the warehouse/laboratory, Rico felt an elation go through him that was shocking both in its intensity and in its sexuality.

"How much longer before we start doing live experiments?"

"At least two months, though we're trying our level best to shorten that time."

"And it'll be as deadly as you said it will be?"

"More than that." The scientist looked at Rico and smiled. "Before anyone even knows that there's a pandemic, tens of thousands—if not in fact hundreds of thousands—will be infected. And they'll infect more people, who will infect more people, who will infect more. The cycle will continue indefinitely. The governments of the world will be helpless against the spread of the disease." The scientist shivered as though in a state of sexual excitement. "There won't be enough room in the morgues. There won't be enough coffins to bury the dead. They'll have to burn the dead in mass crematoriums. They'll have corpses stacked up like cord wood."

Rico could feel his cock start getting hard. Dead Americans stacked like cord wood? Could anything get better than that?

"Keep working," Rico said to the scientist. "You and the other two can count on an additional one hundred thousand dollars in American currency within the next two weeks.

You'll get it in cash, just the way you like it."

"Thank you, Señor Santiago. We will double our efforts to show our appreciation."

"Do that." His tone suggested he wasn't convinced. "When I give up-front money, I expect results.

Now Rico had a decision to make. He could unleash the virus on a major, very crowded, condensed city. A place like Hong Kong, where the people all live shoulder-to-shoulder. But that wasn't the only city he'd poison. He'd wait until the people started falling over in the streets without enough ambulances to cart them away, then he'd let wealthy countries like the United States, England, France, Germany, Switzerland . . . he'd let them know that if they didn't pay his ransom, he'd infect their cities. They'd have thirty days to make their decision. Pay the money, or watch their citizens die in droves. Especially in the United States.

Svetlana studied the body posture of the Santiago brothers as they stepped out of the warehouse, and she liked what she saw. Their heads were high, their shoulders square, and each had a slight grin on his face. Whatever had been said to them in the warehouse was what they wanted to hear. And those were the words they didn't want her to hear.

Svetlana felt a lightning bolt of confidence go through her entire body. They had allowed her to hear schemes of corruption, embezzlement, price gouging, and other highly profitable and highly illegal activities—and they hadn't concerned themselves with keeping any of that a secret. But they had kept whatever their business was in the warehouse an absolute secret. And the warehouse was where they stationed armed guards carrying military-grade assault rifles.

The driver opened the rear door for Rico. As he got in, Svetlana switched to the rearward facing bench seat. She smiled warmly at Rico. Tomas got in the seat beside his brother. To look into his eyes was to look into a cauldron of lust and other emotions that Svetlana didn't want to think too much about.

"How did it go?" Svetlana asked excitedly, playing her role. "Can we go back to your beautiful home now and stop working for the day?"

Tomas looked at Rico and raised his eyebrows, then gave his shoulders a slight hunch. He was playing the beta to his brother's alpha.

Slowly, Rico's gaze slid from Tomas over to Svetlana. He looked first at her face, then down to her breasts, and lastly, to her legs, much of which were exposed below her skirt's hem.

"All work and no play would make Rico a very dull boy." He touched the intercom button on the center console and said to his driver-bodyguard, "There's been a slight change in plans. We're going back home."

With concern in his voice, the bodyguard behind the limousine's steer wheel asked, "Anything wrong? You want me to step on it?"

Svetlana shook her head and put a mysterious glint in her eyes. "The windows are all blacked out. Go through the nice sections of Mexico City for a little bit. I want to be naughty and look out the window while you do things to me, and those people won't know what I'm doing just twenty feet away. Do that for me, and then we can go home. When we're home, I'll do anything you want." She leaned forward and put her hand warmly on Rico's knee. "We've all got some unfinished business, and since you've cancelled your appointment, we're in no hurry. You can have me for as long as you want me."

"I'm really beginning to like the way you think."

Tomas reached over the console and tapped his brother's forearm. "Better call the bank and let them know the meeting's been cancelled."

"Good decision."

As Rico reached inside his suitcoat pocket to get to his phone, Tomas reached out for Svetlana. He wrapped his fingers around her slender wrist, holding her more tightly than necessary. Tomas looked straight into her eyes, and now Svetlana understood what emotion was going through him besides lust.

"I reached for you earlier, and you pushed me away." Tomas got out of his seat, crouching and turning in the big limousine until he was sitting beside Svetlana. There was plenty of room for just the two of them.

Svetlana tried to pull her wrist out of Tomas's grasp, but he only held her more tightly. She could hear Rico now talking on his telephone, but she couldn't pay attention to what he was saying. Not when Tomas was as menacing as he was.

"I don't usually let women push me away," Tomas said, his voice holding a nasty quality to it. "For you, I made an exception. Women are *never* allowed to make me make exceptions."

Well, obviously I did . . . you arrogant prick.

"I'm sorry." She looked into his dark, glittering eyes, then down at the hand that was holding her wrist very tightly. "I guess I just wasn't thinking. I'm sorry. It'll never happen again."

"Damned right it won't." He started pulling on her wrist. At first Svetlana resisted, but then she thought better of it.

"Svetlana, you've got a long day and night ahead of you. I promise you that."

She allowed Tomas to pull her until she was face-down over his lap, her pelvis over his crotch, her upper body on the seat cushions, her knees bent with the toes of her stilettos touching the opposite side window.

She looked at Rico. He was holding a conversation with someone, but she could tell that most of his concentration was on what his little brother was doing to her. Judging by the look in his eyes, Rico approved very much.

Svetlana felt the hem of her skirt get pulled up slowly. Her heartrate accelerated. When, finally, her skirt was bunched at the small of her back, she clenched her teeth.

You can take this, Svetlana. This isn't the first time you've been spanked and then fucked.

She felt Tomas place his hand on her bottom and squeeze gently, almost romantically. It was a polar opposite of the suppressed violence that she had seen in his eyes. He began stroking her legs with his whole hand, not just his fingertips. He caressed her from the calves, up her legs, past the tops of her stockings, to the juncture her thighs. He rubbed her pussy lightly.

"You wear pretty panties."

"Thank you. I'd hoped you'd like them."

His fingers slid beneath the waistband of her lingerie. He moved his hand from side to side, caressing her bottom with the backs of his fingers. Then the fingers clenched into a fist, and an instant later, her panties were ripped from her body. She felt the cloth bite into her flesh as the fabric fought to keep from tearing, but the panties were very sheer, and they gave way to brute strength.

"When panties get in my way, I remove them. And I do it however I want to. Is that clear?"

Svetlana nodded, but she dared not to speak.

"I asked you a question. Is that clear?"

"Yes."

"When I ask you a question, I always expect an immediate answer." He chuckled malevolently. "And you'd better hope like hell that it's the answer I want to hear."

He's psycho. He's not a Dom disciplining his submissive, he's a sadist doing what he loves the most — inflicting pain.

He spanked her, and the first time his palm came down on her ass cheek, there was a loud *smack* that reverberated through the cabin of the limousine, and Svetlana flinched very hard. She cried out in surprise and pain. After that first slap, he stroked his palm over her cheeks for several seconds. Then he delivered the second swat, just as hard.

He doesn't know enough that he's supposed to start soft and then get gradually more and more forceful. That way his sub has time to adjust. Her lip curled, and she was grateful that he couldn't see it. *He's just not very good at this.*

Smack. Smack. Smack.

Svetlana thought her tush getting spanked sounded like machinegun fire inside the limousine.

Rico said, "Easy, brother. You've already taken her very close to her limit."

Who would have thought that Rico would ever be the voice of reason?

Her bottom was stinging, and Svetlana was certain it was flame-red after what had been done to her. A shiver of fear went through her when she thought about how long this lesson in submission might last.

Chapter Thirteen

My God, what an ass. He had thought that of other women before, but there was only one word for Svetlana's backside. *That's a perfect ass.*

He ran his right hand back and forth over the mounds. When the spanking had started, he had turned her buns to a nice, healthy pink. But now her ass showed signs of a spanking that had been delivered with righteous gusto. What had been a pale tush was now one that was hot to the touch, and really quite red.

He ran his right hand over her thigh, savoring the touch of her stockings. He had sufficient experience in such matters that he knew they were silk, and not some silk substitute, like lesser women wore.

Gliding his hand up the inside of her left leg, he went to the top of her leg, then reached farther, using the side of his index finger to test her readiness. He was a little surprised at how wet she felt.

I knew she'd like it.

Tomas rarely doubted himself, and he sure as hell wasn't going to doubt himself on his ability to know how to treat a woman to get her sexually aroused and willing to fuck.

He slipped the tip of his middle finger between the pink-lipped labia, inserting just to the first knuckle. Svetlana made a soft sound in her throat, causing Tomas's cock to get just a little harder as it pressed against Svetlana's belly through several layers of clothing. He pulled out, then pushed back in, a little deeper this time.

With his left hand, he pushed his fingers through her long, honey-blonde hair at the back of her head, and clenched them into a fist. He pulled slowly, forcing Svetlana's head up. He heard her make a struggling sound as her head was forced farther back on her shoulders, and her neck grew taut.

Tomas tried to say something, but he couldn't find the right words to convey the contempt he had for any woman who would deprive him of any pleasure he wanted. He believed with all his heart that, as a Santiago, it was his right — nothing that wasn't due him — to take whoever and however any woman he wanted. And that was the way things were supposed to be . . . and if they weren't, then something was terribly wrong and should be immediately righted.

He very slowly pushed Svetlana off his lap until she was on her knees in the limousine, her face pale but her cheeks flushed.

I always get what I want.

This awareness almost made him break out in song.

The senior guard saw the three men approaching the warehouse, and pegged them right away as winos who were no doubt looking for some place where they could finish their jugs of cheap wine, then sleep it off while laying on a couple pieces of cardboard.

This warehouse district was mostly abandoned, so they'd have plenty of privacy. But the guard knew his employers. The Santiago brothers would never allow three drunks to stay anywhere near the warehouse. The guard didn't know what was going on in the warehouse, but whatever it was, it had to be something important, because only two other warehouses were being used, and neither of those had guards posted.

The three drunks were still thirty yards away, and the guard considered stepping forward so they wouldn't get too close, then decided against it. It just wouldn't do to be accused of abandoning his post by the Santiago brothers.

The guard was a little surprised, as the drunks staggered closer, that all three of them were gringos. Each one carried a large bottle that was big enough to have a handle on it, and each man had a backpack slung over one shoulder. Despite the heat, they were all wearing heavy coats, as people of their ilk often did. And all three of them wore stockings caps, instead of some cooler type of headwear.

When they were fifteen feet away, the guard said, "That's enough. Get the hell out of here. Go piss your pants somewhere else."

He saw the move — the simultaneous action that was identical with all three — as they reached inside their heavy coats and extracted big-bore pistols with a silencer attached to each muzzle.

He felt the first bullet hit him in the stomach. His partner didn't even feel that much because he was shot through the heart and died instantly. A half-second later, the next bullet punched through his body and went through his heart.

Svetlana was on her knees in the limousine, and she could feel the long, slender heels of her shoes digging into the cheeks of her ass.

"Come closer," Tomas said as he struggled with the zipper of his fly. "Show me some sweet love."

He got his erection out through the fly, then began unbuckling his belt and opening his slacks. She was an Omega Force field agent, and she knew what her responsibilities were. In complete opposition to her feelings, Svetlana looked into Tomas's glittering eyes, smiled, and nodded. Not only did she know what Omega Force expected of her, she knew what the Santiago brothers wanted from her.

Very slowly, she wrapped her fingers around the shaft of

his erection, holding him firmly, but not too tightly. Not like he had held her wrists — with such strength that it bordered on pain.

"This has been a long time in coming," she said, a half-smile on her lips as she began stroking him.

Svetlana felt her dress being raised. She looked over her should at Rico. He had moved so that he was almost directly behind her. Saucily, she winked at him, then turned around to face Tomas again.

"Still angry with me?" she asked.

He shook his head. "Once you've been punished, I like to forgive and forget." He kicked his feet out a little more, surrounding Svetlana's kneeling body with his thighs, then put his palm on top of her head and pushed down.

I'll bet you never forget anyone who's ever made you unhappy. I'll bet you've never forgiven anyone who you believe has done you wrong.

She kissed the plump crown of his cock twice, licked it twice, then pushed her lips over the knob. She tried to stop, to take only the head between her lips, but Tomas used enough strength that she had no choice but to take his hard cock to the opening of her throat.

He held her there, immobile, trapped, his cockhead at the entrance to her throat, keeping her on the verge of gagging, because she wasn't one of those women who could swallow a cock whole.

She was struggling against her gag reflex when she felt Rico reach around her body and make quick work of unbuttoning her blouse and unfastening the clasp between the cups of her brassiere. An instant later, the moment her breasts were free, he had both of them in his hands. He firmly but skillfully squeezed them, hefting them as though measuring their weight. Svetlana would have taken pleasure in the caresses had she not been squirming on her knees, fighting against the natural instinct to choke.

Finally, when she could tolerate no more of Tomas's cruelty — and that's what it was, cruelty, not lust — she took both of her palms and slapped Tomas's thighs as hard as she could.

He released the hold he had on her, and was chuckling with great amusement when Svetlana straightened immediately. Her eyes were watery from the strain. She cleared her throat and coughed a half dozen times from behind her fist.

When she could finally speak again, she looked Tomas in the eyes and said with conviction, "Just remember, pretty boy, if you ever do anything like that to me again, I'll eat your balls for breakfast."

Tomas chuckled again, and Svetlana's rage grew hotter.

"Are you so sure you want to put your cock between my sharp teeth again? Sure, I'll be dead afterward . . . but your cock will only be an inch long, and all that it'll be good for is to take a piss."

There was only so much she was going to tolerate in the service of her country. Period.

Rico captured both of her nipples between his fingers and thumbs, and Svetlana angrily batted his hands away.

"Now the only way you're going to fuck me is if you apologize. And you've got to do it in such a manner that I believe every word you say. Because if I don't believe you, the two of you are going to miss out on the hottest fuck you've ever had in your lives." She crossed her arms over her breasts. "So the call is yours to make. It's your decision, but you damned sure are going to play by my rules."

For the next three minutes, two men who hadn't said *I'm sorry* to anyone in years spoke the words of boys forced to do penance in church by an elderly nun with no sense of humor regarding sex-jokes shouted at young virginal girls in Catholic girl uniforms.

The Santiago brothers didn't *actually* get down on their knees — there wasn't enough room for that — but *spiritually* they did.

Finally, after giving them both long, hard looks—particularly at Tomas—with an impish quality in her tone, Svetlana said, as though she was announcing the beginning of a NASCAR race, "Let the games begin. Gentlemen, start your engines."

So hungry were the Santiagos for Svetlana that they didn't actually take off their clothes, they simply opened their slacks to free that part of them which dictated so many of their decision in life.

Svetlana licked slowly around the head of Tomas's cock, then down the shaft until she reached his balls. She licked them, then, as she felt Rico rubbing the crown of his cock against the lips of her pussy, she murmured, "Nice and deep, but not all at once."

As she tucked Tomas's egg-shaped testicle between her lips to make it warm and wet and give Tomas pleasure, she shivered as a second cock, very hard and moderately-sized, forced her body to open.

It's a strange feeling to have two cocks in my body at the same time. She thought back to a time not long ago, when this mission had first started, when she'd gone airtight by taking three cocks in her body into her body simultaneously—and those cocks belonged to men she had met only a few hours earlier. *Three is even stranger than two. By a lot.*

Despite the men she was pleasuring with her mouth and pussy—and the Santiago brothers had few redeeming qualities other than looks and charm, because nobody who looked at their character or behavior would find anything that any decent human being would find laudable—she could feel her libido warming up, her pussy getting wetter and more sensitive, and when she thought of it, she discovered that she was sucking Tomas's cock with more enthusiasm than she had just a minute earlier.

Her mouth was full of Tomas's hard flesh when Svetlana

heard Rico say, "I like the garter belt and stockings. Women who are sexy should dress sexy."

Since she was unable to respond verbally to the compliment, Svetlana waited until Rico's pelvis was pressed tight against her buns and every inch of his cock was being warmed in her cunt, and then she gave her hips a firm, erotic side-to-side shake. She heard Rico's groan, and it was all she needed to know that he approved.

She was rocking slowly back and forth, causing one cock to retreat from her body while the other invaded, when she heard the chirping sound of Rico's cell phone.

You jackass. Don't you dare answer that.

"Hello?" she heard him say, and whatever slight amusement she might have been enjoying with this encounter evaporated like fog in the sun. It took just seconds for this to be simply another assignment for Omega Force. "You're sure it's our building? They all pretty much look the same there." He withdrew completely from Svetlana and sat in his usual forward-facing seat next to the console. "Are the fire trucks there?" Again a pause as something was being explained to Rico. Svetlana sat upright in the seat, and now she and Tomas were listening carefully to what Rico was saying.

"How did you find out about it so soon?" Svetlana heard the suspicion in Rico's tone. "Oh, yes, that's right. I'm the one who bought you the police and fire department scanners, aren't I? Well, keep the phone with you. I'll be in touch." He ended the telephone conversation, then touched the intercom button to his chauffer and said, "Back to the laboratory. Go fast, but we don't want the police stopping us."

Tomas asked, "What was that all about?"

"The laboratory is on fire."

Svetlana asked, "Laboratory?"

Rico gave her a fierce, hateful look. "The warehouse where we just were. My man said the flames are a hundred meters high."

When they got to the mouth of the alley that led to the warehouses, there was already one large fire truck on the scene. Svetlana could hear the wail of many more sirens—both police and fire department.

"Shit. It's a total loss. If the scientists were in there, I'm going to have to start all over from scratch. I'm back to the very beginning."

Tomas made a growling sound in his throat. "It's this bitch. She sold us out." He launched at Svetlana's throat, but Rico grabbed him sharply by the collar and pulled him backward and to the side. Looking first at Svetlana, then at Rico, he said through clenched teeth, "She's fucking set us up, can't you see that?"

"Think about it," Rico said, his tone now placating. "If she was going to betray us, why would she still be with us? Why . . . after she'd turned traitor? She doesn't know a fucking thing about what was going on in that warehouse. Wouldn't she run like hell? She was fucking us when the fire got started." He sighed heavily. "That's millions and millions down the drain, and now I've got to start from square one."

Rico looked at Svetlana, his features rigid, his eyes cold. "My brother thinks you sold us out, and he wants to kill you with his own bare hands. You wouldn't be the first cunt he's fucked and then strangled, all in the same hour. So this is what's going to happen. We're going back to the hotel and you're going to immediately pack those big fucking suitcases you've got. I'll have one of my men drive you to the airport. And after that, you're going to take the first flight that's leaving Mexico City, and you're never coming back here again. If I see you, I'll let my brother fuck you, then strangle you. Got that?"

"Got that."

Havana, Cuba

Svetlana watched a glorious sunrise as she enjoyed her breakfast of eggs, sausage, toast, and coffee. She even splurged on her diet and ordered a mimosa, that magnificent morning cocktail of orange juice and champagne.

Jefferson Burke would surely have questions for her, and she wondered just how severe her punishment would be when she was debriefed by him.

She smiled. Burke was magnificent at all times, but especially when he was administering punishment.

The End

You may also enjoy the following from eXtasy Books Inc:

Deadly Secrets
Robin Gideon

Excerpt

The mansion in the cove was surrounded by an eight-foot-high white marble wall. The original owner had been a member of the New York Mafia, and he'd been more than merely paranoid for his safety, since he had ordered the murders of enough of his former associates, enemies, and friends, to have an on-going "contract" on his head.

As it turned out, the mobster had been safe and protected within the marble walls of his Florida Keys retreat. But his taste for Chinese cuisine was his undoing. He'd been hunched over a heaping plate of sub gum chow mien in a tiny Chinese restaurant when a lone gunman put a .45 automatic to the back of the mob kingpin's head and pulled the trigger.

The current owner of the residence—which included a main house with five bathrooms, five bedrooms, a ballroom large enough to accommodate a party of one hundred comfortably, and three separate fireplaces that had been converted to gas within the past decade—enjoyed the privacy the marble wall gave him more than the protection.

He should have been more concerned with his protection.

Four men and one slender woman, all wearing camouflaged uniforms, slipped quietly over the marble wall. Each soldier was equipped with a Colt Police Positive .38 Special, fitted with a silencer and loaded with hollow-point bullets that had been made into "dum-dums" by having an "X" filed into each one. Upon impact the bullets didn't merely mushroom, they splintered into small segments. The woman did not carry a pistol. Instead, she had in her back pocket a black-handled, stiletto-bladed switchblade. It was her weapon of choice. She preferred her killing to be done up close and with a personal touch.

The secluded mansion's owner was an English gentleman named Sir Malcomb Sitwell. His family — a wife and two sons — owned three cats but no dogs. The cats, upon discovering the intruders, quietly crept to safe shadows, concerned only with their own welfare as the Sitwells slept.

The maid, an elderly immigrant from Germany who often had trouble sleeping throughout the night, had taken two sleeping pills at midnight, afraid that her chronic insomnia would afflict her. She was dreaming of her childhood home in Munich when Jacques entered her bedroom. The room was far removed from the other bedrooms, separated not because of her social status compared to the Sitwells, but because of the volume at which she snored.

Jacques paused a moment to look at the old woman. He waited a second. No more than that. He aimed his Police Positive at her forehead and squeezed the trigger. The long silencer reduced the pistol's roar to a hiss. The hollow-point dum-dum, upon striking the maid's skull, fragmented into four separate pieces of lead and copper. The old woman's head literally exploded.

In other rooms in the mansion, victims were dispatched in similar fashion. Neither of Sir Malcomb's sons heard a thing as they were executed while sleeping.

Sir Malcomb had retired while in his late forties from the

British military. He had bravely served his twenty years, and when he met a wealthy American widow, he moved from London to Florida without remorse. Peace, love, and family contentment had dulled what had for many years been battle-honed senses.

Jacques, Arturo, Deiter, and Petyr were all in the bedroom when Sir Malcomb was shaken awake, a large gloved hand over his mouth to prevent him from making even a sound. Jacques looked into Sir Malcomb's eyes and put a gloved finger to his own lips, indicating silence. Then Sir Malcomb was assisted out of the bed while his wife slept peacefully.

In the library, Juanita extracted from a canvas pouch a bottle of vodka. It was one hundred proof. She opened the bottle, breaking the seal, and pointed toward the overstuffed chair near the fireplace.

"What's the meaning of this?" Sir Malcomb asked, finally finding his voice.

The uniformed soldiers said nothing. Juanita extended the vodka bottle.

"Take this. Drink."

"No."

"Drink it," Juanita said quietly. "If you don't, we'll kill your wife."

The defiance drained quickly out of Sir Malcomb. His eyes darted left and right as he assessed the situation, calculating his chances of fighting back successfully.

"What are you worried about?" Juanita asked. "If we wanted you dead, your brains would be on the floor. Now take the bottle and drink. Finish it all and nothing will happen to you. I promise."

Malcomb took the bottle and brought it to his lips. It took him almost five minutes to drink the entire pint of liquor.

Deiter stepped into the library. He nodded his head, saying nothing. When he did, the faintest smile curled Juanita's lips.

"Very good," she said. She placed the bottle on the carpeted floor beside Malcomb. "Just sit there now. Everything will be just fine in a matter of minutes."

Juanita watched as the alcohol began clouding Malcomb's brain. She saw him blinking his eyes as he tried to clear his vision. It was a pleasure to watch the capitalist trying to intellectualize his way past the alcohol that was fogging and diluting his reasoning. Three times Juanita walked past him, moving just a little closer each time. He stopped watching her carefully.

Juanita brought out a second bottle. She opened the vodka, breaking the seal. This time she did not hand the bottle to Sir Malcomb. Rather, she put it to his lips and forced his head back. He knew what was expected, and gulped the clear, fiery liquid as best he could. Vodka dribbled over his chin and down his neck, only to get soaked up in his fine silk pajamas.

"That should do it," Juanita said when the last of the second bottle of vodka had, quite literally, been poured down Sir Malcomb's throat.

She waited until she was on the verge of losing consciousness before she took the .38 Special from Deiter. She unscrewed the silencer and then placed the weapon in Sir Malcomb's relaxed hand. He said something, or at least tried to say something. Saliva trickled from the corner of his mouth.

Juanita turned the weapon inside Malcomb's hand so that the muzzle touched his temple. He started to protest, fighting against the young Mexican woman with the fathomless black eyes.

The Colt Police Positive roared, the deafening noise of the .38 Special being fired echoing off the walls. The force of the fragmenting round bursting through hard skull and soft brain tissue tossed Sir Malcomb out of the chair. The left side of his head had disintegrated.

About the Author

Robin Gideon is the author of over 50 novels and novellas in paperback form and for e-publishers. She is currently writing erotic action-adventure stories starring the secret agent Svetlana Simonov exclusively for eXtasy Books. She was the featured author on the nationally syndicated TV series CBS Sunday Morning. She loves hearing from her readers, and can be reached at: robin.gideon@ymail.com.